Strawberry Moon

ALSO BY KAREN ENGLISH

Francie

Strawberry Moon

KAREN ENGLISH

FARRAR STRAUS GIROUX • NEW YORK

Copyright © 2001 by Karen English
All rights reserved
Distributed in Canada by Douglas & McIntyre Ltd.
Printed in the United States of America
Designed by Vincenzo Longo
First edition, 2001
10 9 8 7 6 5 4 3 2 1

Library of Congress Cataloging-in-Publication Data
English, Karen.
    Strawberry moon / Karen English.— 1st ed.
        p. cm.
    Summary: While driving to Auntie Dot's house, Junie tells her
children about spending fifth grade there during her parents' separation
many years earlier, when finding a best friend seemed almost as
important as seeing her mother again.
    ISBN 0-374-47122-3
    [1. Moving, Household—Fiction. 2. Friendship—Fiction.
3. Aunts—Fiction. 4. African Americans—Fiction. 5. Los Angeles
(Calif.)—Fiction.] I. Title.

PZ7.E7232 St 2001
[Fic]—dc21
                                                            00-68124

TO THE MEMORY OF MY FATHER, ALEX,

AND MY AUNT ALBERTA

Strawberry Moon

Imani looks up at the moon—full and round—and the upside-down Big Dipper—or maybe it's the Little Dipper. Fields race by while the moon stays in place.

"How long before we get there?" she says, putting a little whine in her voice. Her mother won't answer. She doesn't answer questions while she drives. It's her thinking time, unless she has something she wants to talk about. Imani turns to Blair.

"That's a strawberry moon," she says, pointing out the window. "That's me and Mommy's moon because we were both born in June. You were born in March during a worm moon."

Blair's eyes get big. He's always easy to stir up. "I was not!"

"Don't tease, Imani," her mother shoots over her shoulder. "I'd like some peace and quiet right about now."

It's going to be a long trip—on the usual dark, monotonous highway dotted only by rest stops and gas station/mini-stores and the winding red line of taillights.

They're headed to Imani's great-aunt's house in Los Angeles. Mommy's famous Auntie Dot. Only this time Daddy won't be flying down later so they can all drive back together and stop at Solvang and Big Sur and the aquarium at Monterey. Mommy is having a "difficult time" at home. Imani heard her say these words when she passed Mommy's room last week. Mommy had been on the phone with her best friend, her back to the door.

Maybe they'd all—minus Daddy—pack up and move to L.A., she had said into the receiver, her voice angry and low, but Imani had heard. "I can stay with my aunt and see how it goes." It didn't seem like a very thought-out plan. To Imani, it seemed haphazard.

"I'm going to be bored," Blair says out of the blue.

Imani thumps her head on the car window, feeling its vibrations through her teeth and a tingle in her nose. It's bothersome, but she's in a mood to feel bothered physically, as well.

"Boredom's a good thing," their mother says in her new false, glib way.

Imani rolls her eyes.

"Auntie Dot's TV's black-and-white," Blair says. "It hurts my eyes."

"Don't watch," Mommy says.

"Are there any kids on her block yet?"

"I don't know."

"Who will I play with?"

"Play with Imani."

Imani and Blair look at each other with disgust, then aim their faces out the window. What's the use?

Suddenly out of the quiet, her mother says in a low voice, "I remember when I first came to Los Angeles."

"Tell us that story, Mommy," Imani says, feeling suddenly drowsy and forgiving. She's heard the "Mommy" stories a million times, about when her mother was a kid and had to wear dresses with a tie in the back and piping around the collar, and how girls couldn't wear pants to school. Kids had school clothes and school shoes that had to be polished every night and placed on newspaper to dry. Mommy's stories are bizarre and entertaining and always make Imani feel relieved she doesn't have to live them herself.

She looks over at Blair with his cheek pressed against the back of the seat, his eyes closed, his thumb in his mouth.

"I was the same age as you, Imani. My mother and father had separated." Mommy pauses, and the word "separated" hovers in the air for a moment. "Me and your uncle Junior and my daddy came out to California to live with Auntie Dot."

"I want to hear about it again," Imani says.

"Well—it was like being deposited on the moon. I'd never known anything like California. I was completely disoriented."

Imani thinks about this. It's always hard to see her mother little and lost.

"I want to hear the Mavis story," Blair says, taking his thumb out of his mouth.

"I'll get to that."

In a calm, quiet voice, Imani's mother begins:

"To me, California was another country. The trees were tall and skinny, and houses had roofs like broken pottery. I remember sitting in the back of your great-uncle Melvin's Oldsmobile and imagining someone on his hands and knees scrubbing the smooth, broad, neat streets leading away from the airport. I remember thinking California had a different light, clean and bleached, so unlike the dappled light that fell through the overarching trees on my Chicago street. Blinding, nearly. I didn't like it at all. And the mountains . . . I was used to flat land."

Imani closes her eyes to see Auntie Dot's street through her mother's eyes at ten. Browning Avenue, she thinks. The name reminds her of flour being browned in a pan for gravy. Mommy's voice breaks into her thoughts.

"And Auntie Dot. I couldn't be sure she'd be a friend. She was my daddy's big sister. Her rich brown skin, the tiny moles speckling her cheek and going down her neck fascinated me. We were all yellow people. I was proud of her color because I knew beneath our bland paleness was the blueprint for all the spicy variations. We had range—even if it hadn't come out in me or Junior.

"There was nothing subtle about Auntie's clothes. That day she wore a dress with big splashy flowers and grape-size pearl earrings, things my mother never would have worn. But there was something comforting about her boldness. After a cool peck on my cheek at the airport, she leaned back and squinted down at me as if she knew me already. Knew my heart and soul.

"We drove down those pristine streets and I snuck peeks at her from the back seat. My future was in her hands—not my Uncle Melvin's. He was easy-going and there was no mystery about him. I knew where I stood with him as soon as he pulled a quarter out from behind my ear and dropped it into my palm. It was Auntie I was worried about. What must she think about us just dropping into her life, kaboom? Surely we were an intrusion.

"My mother had let us go. Easily, from what I could gather. I remembered walking across the tarmac with Daddy and Junior to board the plane and looking back at her. She was waving cheerfully behind the big glass pane as if we were heading off for a vacation in Hawaii and she would be joining us later.

"That year Daddy turned silent and Mommy would become this chirpy voice on the telephone sounding squeezed through a straw. If my mother could let me go, then I could let her go, as well.

"That's how I began my year with Auntie Dot. That's how I began my year of troubles: letting my mother go."

We pulled up in front of Auntie's bungalow on Browning Avenue with the wide cement porch and big stone posts flanking the steps, and I thought: How am I going to live here? I sat there in the back seat, a knot growing in my throat. Of course, Daddy, acting as if nothing bad was going on in our lives, hopped out, dashed around the car to the trunk, and cheerfully started helping Uncle Melvin with the luggage.

Uncle Melvin scared me a tiny bit with his sagging face. He'd had a stroke and it had left him with a shuffling gait and a face that hung down like a beagle's on one side. When he talked, only the good side moved. But he was kind and understanding—I came to learn—and always gently in my corner.

Loaded down with all our suitcases, Daddy, Uncle Melvin, and Junior trudged up the front walkway with me behind carrying only my little overnight case and my stuffed dog, Barky. I knew I was too old for stuffed animals but I didn't care. I'd had him since I was three and I did not plan on giving him up. Not now.

I felt as if we were all under the watchful eyes of Auntie's neighbors. Every last one of them. Peeking through the cracks in their curtains.

Then I saw it. Auntie's monster flower. It was so prickly bright, I jumped—making everyone laugh. It looked to be leaping out of its plot of soil, its thick, sharp, pointed leaves aimed right at me, poised to take a nip out of my arm. I backed up, giving it a wide berth. Everyone thought it was the funniest thing, my being afraid of a flower. I felt like crying. I slithered into the house, humiliated. I was not off to a good start.

For the next few weeks I avoided the flower. I would leave for school through the side door off the dining room. When I got home, I would enter through the back door, which Auntie always left open even when she was next door visiting with Miss Ida, our neighbor Mr. Bell's sister. When Junior insisted we play Old Maid on the porch, I always made sure I sat facing that flower. If I didn't, I could feel the pressure of its presence on my back—as if it was just waiting to take a bite out of my neck.

One hot October Saturday, I lay on my back on Auntie's lawn looking through the pattern of the fat leaves of her avocado tree. I was sulking and missing my mother and feeling everything was strange and unlike Chicago and therefore stupid. Few trees changed colors in dumb Los Angeles. There was no anticipation of winter coming in the flat, lukewarm air.

Mr. Bell, next door, was trimming his hedges in short, precise whacks that had a satisfying, purposeful sound. Snip, snip. I lost myself in the rhythm of it. I sat up on my elbows and watched the shears scissor across the top of the hedge. The blades were long and narrow and let Mr. Bell do his damage at a distance. If I had those shears I would slice the head off Auntie's bird-of-paradise—I'd since learned the monster's name. One, two, three, my problem would be solved. Auntie wanted that plant trimmed back anyway. "It'll be blocking the steps before you know it, Melvin—it's growing fast." I heard her say it again and again. Certainly Auntie must have a pair of those shears.

I pulled myself up and headed for the small detached garage, looking back over my shoulder at Miss Ida Bell's kitchen window.

No one was home. Junior had gone to a matinee with some friends—he always made friends fast and easily. No standing behind the screen door watching the neighborhood kids for him. He'd come right out and ask if he could play, too. Auntie was next door visiting with Miss Ida, Daddy was working overtime, and Uncle Melvin, who had to guard his poor health, was napping.

I stepped through the side door of the garage and stood there a moment, letting my eyes grow accustomed to the dim light. Garden tools hung on protruding metal hooks on a pegboard. Shears just like the ones Mr. Bell was using were within arm's reach, as if they'd been waiting for me all morning—waiting for me to get my idea. "It's about time," they seemed to say.

Carefully, I slipped them off the hook. They were

heavier than I'd imagined. Even with two hands, it was hard to push the blades closed. It was just like me to underestimate a bright idea. Things seemed so simple when you were lying on the grass staring at a bunch of leaves.

I poked my head out the side door, and then quickly scooted up the back steps, through the kitchen, the dining room, the living room, and then out the front door. I shoved the shears under the porch swing, then sat down to plot my next course of action. I hadn't dared look at the bird-of-paradise until I was safely seated far away from it.

It knew what I was planning to do. I could feel it. I bit on my thumbnail and rocked, waiting for the right time and pretending that I wasn't up to anything. The lady across the street was talking to the mailman. They looked over at me suspiciously it seemed. I gazed up at the empty sky, then went to work on my other thumbnail.

Finally, the lady disappeared into her house, and the mailman started moseying up Browning Avenue. With the rash determination of someone taking that first leap into a pool of water, I reached for the shears, leaned forward, and using all my strength, chopped off the ferocious blossom. It dropped into the soil with a thud, its mouth gaping open in agony. Panicking, I raced around the house, though still sensible enough to keep the blades pointed down safely, as I had learned to do in kindergarten when carrying scissors. Back in the garage, I aimed the little ring attached to one of the shears' handles at the protruding wall hook and threw. It caught on the first try, which gave me a boost of confidence: I'd done the right thing.

I crept out of the garage and went inside.

"What were you doing with those gardening shears?"

It was Junior. He'd just come back from the movies and must have seen me running to the garage.

"Nothing."

"You were too doing something. You were *sneaking* into the garage. And you wouldn't be sneaking if you weren't up to something." He turned his tall glass of juice up to his mouth.

I weighed my options, then decided to tell the truth. "I got rid of that awful flower by the porch."

He stopped in mid-gulp and widened his eyes. "Oooh, you gonna get it," he said around a low, throaty chuckle. Then he let go with a loud, hearty laugh. "You gonna get it!" He turned to go, whooping all the way down the hall. I heard his bedroom door softly close and his muffled laugh behind it.

Suddenly, I was stung with fear. I wondered if I could Scotch-tape the dead and now harmless flower head back onto its stem. I peeked through the window over the sink at Miss Ida's. All still and calm, for now.

"Mommy, why would you do something so stupid?"
Imani says.

"Just listen and let me finish. You might learn something."

"Eat those peas, Junie," Auntie said later that day at dinner. I ate a pea and put my mind on something else to ward off the gag reflex. I hated peas. Junior was peering at me over his pile of mashed potatoes. Auntie had returned from Miss Ida's through the kitchen door, which gave me an agonizing temporary reprieve. Daddy was late coming home from working an extra day at the Long Beach Shipyard, so there was only me, Junior, Auntie, and Uncle Melvin sitting at the table. Auntie was keeping Daddy's dinner warm in the oven on a plate covered with a pot lid.

Junior smiled his slick smile.

"What's so funny about those mashed potatoes?" Uncle Melvin said, the words slurring out of one side of his mouth.

"Nothing, Uncle Melvin."

Auntie shot a quick look at Junior, then went back to her slab of roast beef. Dinner continued silently. I had no appetite. Not even for the banana pudding sitting warm on the stove.

Just then, we heard the back door. Soon Daddy walked through the swinging dining-room door. "Hello, all," he said in the fake cheery voice he'd adopted since our move. "How's my family?"

I shrugged, thinking Auntie and Uncle Melvin were not his family. Me, Mommy, and Junior were his family. Why was he pretending? He ducked back into the kitchen to wash his hands at the sink.

Daddy called out, "What happened to your bird-of-paradise, Dot?"

"What do you mean?" she answered.

He came to the table drying his hands on a paper towel. "One of the neighborhood pranksters must have gotten to it. The flower was hacked off. I saw it in the dirt."

Auntie's eyes narrowed. Slowly, she rose from her seat. Uncle Melvin stopped eating for a moment. I sank deeper into my chair, hoping to melt into the worn brocade cushion. Junior was wearing his most wicked, slithery smile now—I'd never seen him look so ugly.

Auntie came back in a flash. "Anyone know what happened to my bird-of-paradise?" She looked directly at me. And because I was under the spotlight of her piercing gaze, I spoke the truth.

"I did it."

Daddy, who'd started in on his roast beef, stopped and looked over at me.

"I was scared of it. I thought it was going to bite me," I said in a rush.

Daddy's face began to contort with disbelief. Auntie's remained completely passive. "Going to bite you?" she asked.

I nodded.

She sat down.

"You thought what?" Daddy said.

I didn't want to repeat something that now sounded dumb even to my own ears.

Daddy turned to Auntie. "I'll try to find you another plant."

"I wish you luck. They can be hard to find," she said.

Daddy then came up with a brilliant idea. "Well, until I do, Junie'll let you hold on to Barky—so she can see how it feels to be without something she likes, too."

I tried to make Daddy look at me. Surely he understood that I knew how it felt to be without. I'd been without since we moved to California. Lately, I'd been trying to calculate the distance between me and my mother in city blocks. Twelve to a mile. Three thousand times twelve.

I could not be without Barky. My mother gave me Barky—when I was four and a half and had the chicken pox and was miserable with the itchy blisters on the soles of my feet, in my ears, even on my eyelids. Barky had seen me through everything. He saw me through the time my best friend, Aja, announced out of the blue that she was no longer my friend. I had to spend recess on a bench reading a book for a month, and each day I'd come home and run for Barky just in time to let out the wail I'd been holding in. I couldn't give up Barky. He was much more valuable than any dumb flower.

"Come on," Daddy said without a bit of heart. "Let's go get him." He led me down the hall and into my room. Numb with grief, I watched him retrieve Barky from his throne on the shelf that once held Auntie's folded yards of fabric. I sank down into my bed sitting on my hands. Was Daddy expecting me to cry? I would *not*. He left the room carrying my dear stuffed friend.

"Grandpa Blair was being mean," Imani says. Her own daddy wouldn't act that way. As soon as they got to Auntie's she was going to call him. She would ask him to come get her. Or at least send plane fare. And Daddy would do it, too. Just because Mommy was mad at him didn't mean Imani had to be.

"Maybe your grandpa wasn't being mean then," Mommy says. "Maybe it just felt like it." She smiles and Imani feels a prick of guilt about her plan. "You know what happened?"

I'd been instructed by Daddy to apologize and pledge sterling behavior from that point on. And I'd done my part at Daddy's urging. I dramatically declined dessert when I was called back to the table, and asked to be excused.

But Barky was returned to me, by Auntie, two days later. When I got back from school that Monday, he was sitting on the shelf in my bedroom. Auntie had understood me more than Daddy had. Daddy saw things in a straight line. Auntie saw them all around.

"Thank you for giving Barky back to me," I said in a near-whisper when I went into the kitchen to formally greet her. Auntie didn't like us to come in from school without giving her a proper "Hello, Aunt Dot. How are you?" She was on the telephone, probably with Miss Ida. They often talked while they prepared their evening meals.

She nodded at me, and I could tell I had a friend in Auntie. I'd have to mind my p's and q's, but she felt for me and she was willing to be kind.

I left the kitchen and went to my room to study my times tables. Miss Dickerson, my teacher, had discovered—to her horror, it seemed—that her students could recite only the easy 5's and 2's without hesitation. I pulled out the 6 table, deciding to start with what was almost too hard. Just then Junior passed my door with something bulging under his jacket. He was silent and secretive in his own way, though I knew with certainty what he was hiding.

His math teacher had called the week before with concerns about Junior's lack of focus. He hadn't done a single homework assignment in two weeks. Daddy took away radio and television privileges, along with his beloved baseball mitt.

Even so, Junior was probably going to play catch over at the house of some new friend he'd made. Junior didn't pay attention to punishments if he could get away with it.

Bring Me the Iron

Junior had his own ways of acting out.

In the mild autumn evenings we'd sit on Auntie's back steps and listen to the train that ran the same time each day. It doesn't run anymore, but at that time L.A. had a lot of trains going everywhere. The clanking reminded me and Junior of Chicago, so almost every night we'd wind up sitting on the porch listening for the familiar whistle.

I knew Junior had been in his own world of woe. He was small for his age and people always looked openly surprised when he told them he was in the ninth grade. He wasn't much taller than I was. Daddy kept assuring him that when he hit his growth spurt he'd shoot up at least six or seven inches overnight.

But looking at Junior then, with his long head and small, narrow shoulders and stick-figure arms, I couldn't see him shooting up at all. I thought it was some fantasy Daddy had, more for his own benefit than Junior's. But it was a sensitive topic—one we weren't supposed to talk about, just as we weren't supposed to say anything about Junior still occasionally wetting the bed.

The amazing, admirable thing about Junior—I admired it because I didn't have this quality in me—was his bravado. He'd swagger into any situation, seemingly without fear. I guess it was the pride of a little man. But he still paid a price, hauling his vulnerabilities around close to the chest. He had no one to talk to. Not Daddy, because Daddy was grooming Junior to be a man like him—showing no emotion, all silence.

"Who's that boy you hang around with at school?" I ventured carefully. Carefully because if you seemed too interested, it could come off as too nosy to Junior. The boy seemed unsavory to me, somehow. He wore drooping chinos and white T-shirts and looked like the lowriders who cruised around the junior high in their Chevys, prowling for junior high school girls. And that boy had straightened hair. We called it a "process." A big no-no in our household.

"He's a friend. Why?"

"I just wondered," I said, trying to sound casual. But I didn't want Junior hanging out with such a person. He wasn't like us. I'd noted his nails were grimy and long, and I'd seen him walking down the street with a cigarette in his mouth just as bold as you please. Junior wasn't that kind of boy. And I didn't want people thinking he was.

"I heard Daddy talking on the phone to Mom," Junior said out of the blue. He kept his eyes straight ahead.

"What were they talking about?"

"I think she was asking about me and you."

"What was she asking?"

"You think I could hear what she was asking?" He got up abruptly then and went into the house. I knew it. Any little thing could set him off. It was always just a matter of time.

One of Junior's favorite pastimes while we were away from our mother was scaring me. He told me he heard noises coming from Auntie's back porch, and how sometimes he could hear the big freezer chest opening and closing on its own.

I protested, of course, said he was making up stories, but something about them scared the bejeebies out of me. As far as I was concerned, as long as I stayed off the back porch at night, it didn't matter whether what he said was true or not.

"Probably mice," I said, not much comforted by my own suggestion.

"Mm," was all Junior would say, raising one eyebrow. "You think so?" He'd cock his head to the side and walk away.

One night Auntie was sitting at the dining-room table making curtains for Miss Ida's back bedroom. When she got in one of her sewing moods, her sewing machine could reside on the dining-room table for days. Junior and I were happy when the table was occupied. Then we could escape the stiffness of the family dinner and eat on TV trays and watch *Lassie* instead, not having to say a word.

While I was sprawled on the floor watching the show, Auntie looked up from her sewing, took a drag on her cigarette—she liked to smoke while she sewed—and said, "Junie, go out to the back porch and bring me the iron." Auntie usually left the ironing board up against the wall, but she always put the iron away. She didn't trust an iron to be stored anywhere but on the back porch on the cool washing machine.

At first I pretended I hadn't heard her, but my heart had nearly stopped. I prayed she'd redirect this request to Junior.

"Junie," Junior said, hardly able to contain himself, "Auntie said go get her the iron."

I looked over at Junior. He was leaning back on his hands, his eyes still on the television screen. There was something menacing in his words. He looked over at me. "Didn't you hear her?"

"Why can't you go get it?"

"Because she asked *you.*"

"Junie . . . ," Auntie said through teeth clenched around a spray of straight pins in her mouth.

"Ma'am?"

"Go get me the iron."

Slowly I got up. Slowly I approached the room. I reached the kitchen and stood in the doorway, looking through the darkness to the back-porch door. It had a glass window in the top half. Behind that window I could sense something crouching.

My mouth dried out. There was no way I could cross that kitchen to the back porch.

"Junie . . ." Auntie's voice bounced off my back.

Just then I heard Junior's voice. "Junie, where's the iron? Auntie needs the iron."

I started to cry.

Junior came then and leaned on the doorjamb, studying my predicament. "Go on. I'll watch you from here."

The switch for the kitchen was over by the stove. Now, there was only a long rectangle of light stretching across the floor from the hallway. "Go on," he repeated nonchalantly. "Nothin's gonna happen to you."

I stepped over the threshold and waited.

"I'm right here," Junior said.

I crept across the speckled linoleum to the midway point of the kitchen. The refrigerator hummed, the faucet dripped, and through the window moonlight cast shadows of tree branches that trembled sinisterly.

"Go on . . ." Junior's voice was now a whisper.

I moved onward to the back door, then looked behind me at Junior. He smiled encouragingly. I went quickly then. But just as my hand grasped the doorknob, just as I began to turn it, Junior let out a blood-curdling scream. He shrank back and slid down the wall to the floor, his eyes bulging.

My heart leaped to my throat. I began to scream and jump in place. Junior, now on the floor, shielded his face, but I could hear a muffled laugh.

I heard Auntie's slapping slippers coming our way. "What on earth . . ."

By then I had collapsed into hysterics. She rushed past me like the wind and threw on the light. I looked around, then stood blinking at the glass window of the back-porch door and the blackness behind it.

Imani looks over at Blair. He's sitting upright, his eyes wide. Imani chuckles to herself softly. Mommy continues.

Slowly Junior got up from the floor. Found out. He was all sober and quiet. Auntie grabbed his arm and pulled him to his toes, which was not hard to do. "Boy, what are you up to?" How quickly she'd assessed the situation.

"Nothin'."

"You in here scarin' this child?"

"No, ma'am." He looked at his feet.

Auntie pulled him toward the door. "You get yourself in the bed." Junior looked horror-stricken. He was going to miss the rest of *Lassie*. "If I'da known she was so scared," Auntie said, "I'da got that iron myself."

Auntie moved past me, snatched the iron off the washing machine, and walked quickly out of the kitchen, leaving me standing there trying to understand what had happened.

I peeked into the back porch. Nothing was there but Auntie's old freezer, the foldout drying rack, her washer, and the clothes hamper. Nothing else. I left the light on in the kitchen.

Passing Junior's room, I spied him lying on his bed on top of his cowboy bedspread, his arms under his head, staring at the ceiling. I'd been in that place before. I knew what he was feeling. He looked over at me with a pouting mouth and accusing eyes. It was all my fault, they said. All his woes, his loneliness, his confusion . . . It was all my fault.

I moved on, feeling a strange guilt, as if in part his feelings were legitimate—as if I did have something to do with his misery. I felt some satisfaction, too. Auntie had taken up for me, in her usual, unpredictable way, when I least expected it.

I wondered why she and Uncle Melvin had never had children of their own. I wondered if she would be as good a mother as she was an aunt.

Later I fell asleep to the start-and-stop rhythm of Auntie's sewing machine.

"Why didn't she ever have kids, Mommy?" Imani asks.

"Later I learned there had been a child, stillborn at eight months. But I never learned why there were no children after that . . .

"You know, Auntie's the one who told me the name of my moon."

Pepper Cake

One Saturday in early December, Auntie was having one of her club meetings. The December meeting was the most important of the year, it seemed. It ushered in the holiday season with a frenzy of activity in preparation for the club's big fund-raising extravaganza. Once a year the club ladies put together a big dinner and auction to raise money for the Children's Home Society on Adams Boulevard. I loved that building. Whenever we'd drive past it, I'd search and search those wide, sloping lawns for orphans. I almost wished I could be an orphan and live in that big white-pillared mansion and be taken care of by a whole regiment of women in starched white uniforms. I never saw any orphans, though. Years later I learned that the building was for administrative purposes only. The pillars, the lawn—all for show.

This event, I guess, gave meaning to all those other meetings throughout the year, which I secretly thought were just an excuse to put on white gloves and hats and eat lots of good food.

That last meeting of the year also gave Auntie a chance to showcase her favorite holiday: Christmas. She had had Daddy and Uncle Melvin drag in the huge aluminum tree from the garage right after Thanksgiving. It came in pieces and had to be assembled. She nagged and nagged them until they had it standing upright in a corner of the living room, where she could decorate it with royal-blue satin balls and lights. She'd seen such a vision in a magazine once and was very impressed. Auntie would just beam when she'd hear, "Dot, that tree sure is something. It's sure spectacular."

I hated that fake tree. I figured it was a California thing. We never *ever* had a fake tree in Chicago. Ours were real and had the most wonderful pine fragrance. Auntie's had no smell at all. She could spray all the pine-scented air freshener she wanted, and it would never smell like Christmas in Chicago, what with the awful metallic *undersmell.*

Auntie loved wreaths. She put a wreath on the front door, on all the living-room windows, and even one on the refrigerator. A plastic one, with prickly imitation holly leaves and poisonous-looking red plastic berries.

She loved outdoor lights, too. They were strewn over everything—all around the porch and on every bush. These gave the porch a magical feeling that I actually liked. I'd planned to ignore Christmas that year. If it couldn't be as it had always been, I'd mentally hold my breath until it passed. Anyway, what kind of December was it with seventy-degree weather and people running around in shirtsleeves?

On top of everything else, I was still almost friendless in Miss Dickerson's class. All the students' old friendships had been sealed in kindergarten, it seemed to me, and I was to have no one in this new place but Eva

Cummings, a plump, eager girl who was hoping I would be the person who would finally depend on her attention. But we ate lunch together in almost utter silence. California may have been sunny and warm, but my world was cold and unpredictable.

On the day of Auntie's holiday meeting, I sat in the kitchen and watched her cook. She often talked on the phone while she worked, stretching the cord all over the kitchen. Sometimes while she chopped and diced, she'd sit on her kitchen stool with the receiver trapped between her head and her shoulder. Then she'd snap her fingers at me and point, and I'd hop up to retrieve whatever it was she couldn't reach.

For this particular meeting Auntie was making her Sock-It-to-Me cake. She was famous for her Sock-It-to-Me cake. Now, here was a time I just slid into trouble without giving it much thought. While Auntie whipped the batter by hand, she sat on her stool talking on the phone to Miss Ida, who was making monkey bread over at her house. I envied my auntie having a best friend right next door—someone to cook with even while a redwood fence separated them.

"Hold on, Ida," Auntie said at one point to go answer the door. She'd been expecting a package that she'd have to sign for. She pushed the bowl to me. "Stir this while I'm gone," she said. When she went out of the room, I stared down into that bowl of cake batter and felt a strange itch to do something naughty. There sat the blue container of Morton salt with the picture of the little girl in a bright yellow raincoat looking like she'd just given her umbrella a twirl—so easily within reach.

Then my eyes drifted to the special container of white pepper on the small spice shelf over the stove. I had to climb onto the stool to get at it. I looked back at the closed kitchen door until I felt safe. Then I hurried to the bowl of batter, opening the pepper container as I crossed the room. I dumped as much of it into the batter as I dared, gave it a stir, and arranged myself into an innocent pose after returning the container to the shelf.

I felt Auntie's eyes on me when she returned, but she merely picked up the receiver and resumed her conversation.

The cake pans were put into the oven and Auntie started on the potato salad. Soon I grew tired of watching and listening. I wandered into the living room to pound out one of my made-up songs on the piano.

"Keep that racket down, Junie," Auntie called out to me.

When the first club member showed up at the door, I went out to the back patio to practice my jacks.

It was a warm day for December, and every window in the dining room was open. I could hear the whoops of laughter and voices spilling over each other excitedly as more and more guests arrived.

Eventually, in the middle of my third time doing six-ies, I heard Miss Marvelle from down the street say, "Well, Dot, isn't it about time you brought out that Sock-It-to-Me cake of yours?" Next I heard chair legs scraping. Someone was making room for Auntie to get it on the table. I stopped practicing.

"I want me a big piece," said Mrs. Johnston. "I'm forgetting all about my diet today."

Excitement stirred my stomach.

I could hear plates and silver clinking. I could hear exclamations over every slice passed around. There was laughter. Then there was silence. Suddenly, an eruption of fierce coughing started up—and calls for water—and sounds of a lot of rushing around—and choked-out words of apology. I listened to it all. I went on to sevensies . . .

. . . Until the back door slammed behind me. "Auntie wants you, Junie," Junior said in a voice that showed he knew I was at the bottom of the commotion. He followed close on my heels.

I pushed through the kitchen door into a room full of women with hankies to their mouths, or sipping glasses of water, their eyes red and watering.

"Just wanted to make sure you had a piece of my special Sock-It-to-Me cake," Auntie said. "Go on out and play," she told Junior. His shoulders slumped with disappointment as he left the room. Auntie squinted down at me with noticeably reddened eyes. Finally, I was frightened.

She held out the cake cut and ready for me. It looked fine, frosted with butter cream on her good china plate. I took it and sat down on the chair by the window. "Go ahead. Take a bite," Auntie ordered.

I took a bite. I tasted pepper immediately. It tickled the back of my throat, gagging me and flooding my eyes with tears. I began to cough and choke and struggle for breath.

All eyes were on me. Some were full of reproach, some filled with utter bewilderment.

"Why, child? Why would you put pepper in the cake I was serving to my company?"

How could I answer when I had no answer? Surely I did not know. It seemed like a fun thing to do at the time. I did not think beyond the doing of it.

"You take that cake into your room and you spend the whole rest of the day and night in there with it. That there"—she pointed her long finger at it—"is your dinner and your breakfast. Now go."

I slunk away. In my room I set the cake on my dresser and went to sit on the bed and think. I looked out the window at Auntie's avocado tree. I could hear kids playing somewhere down the street and wished my room was in front of Auntie's house instead of in the back so I could put faces with the voices I was hearing. The voices of kids having fun. Kids who weren't sitting on their beds—punished.

Later, when I grew hungry, I ate all the icing off the cake. The pepper hadn't invaded the icing. A delicious aroma of chicken frying soon drifted in from the kitchen. Then I could hear the sounds of Daddy, Junior, Auntie, and Uncle Melvin eating dinner. I didn't feel as if an injustice was being done to me. Incredibly, I wasn't resentful. I just felt tremendously sad. I kept thinking about Miss Dickerson's class and the fact that I had no best friend yet. And about my mother.

Finally, it was dark and the moon was big and round and filling the sky. I stared at it, wishing I was there in that lit-up place. I was drifting to sleep when I heard someone tap on the door.

"Junie?" Auntie said, stepping into the room.

"Ma'am?"

"I need you to come with me." She turned and started down the hall. "It's chilly out," she said over her shoulder. "Put on a sweater and let's go out to the porch."

After a moment I got off the bed, slipped into a sweater, and followed her.

As I passed the kitchen, I looked deep into it, noting with disappointment it was closed for the night, dishes done, everything put away, and now humming a late-night, shut-down hum.

We sat quietly on the porch swing. It was strangely clear for a winter night—a California night, so close to the Pacific Ocean.

Auntie looked up at the moon.

"See that moon? See how big it is? That there's the long-nights moon."

"The what?"

"The long-nights moon. What the Indians called December's full moon."

"Why?"

"That's how they saw time."

I thought about this. I knew how I saw time. And how my best friend Aja in Chicago saw time. We were the only two people who saw time in a kind of graphic way, we'd decided. Mine was like a long oval track with December on the right end of the oval and January stretching long across the top. I suppose January seemed long and tedious and without personality to me and never the true beginning of things. March was the start of the left-sided curve. May was in the middle and June started the long bottom part. I don't know when I'd started seeing the year laid out like that. But it had been with me all my life. Aja's was up and down like the Chutes and Ladders game.

"Now, you know what your moon is?"

"Mine?"

"Yes, child. You have a moon."

"What's mine?"

"You were born in June. Yours is the strawberry moon."

"My moon is the strawberry moon?" That had such a beautiful sound to it, I wanted to cry. Strawberry moon. She might as well have dropped a diamond into my hand—giving me the name of my very own moon. I was hungry and I wasn't about to get any of that fried chicken everyone had had for dinner, but those two words were delicious enough for me to eat. Strawberry moon. Something to ponder. I didn't feel as sad then. I felt almost excited.

We sat there a little while longer. Soon Auntie said it was time for me to go to sleep. We'd done enough moon-watching for the night. But still it shone through the bedroom window bathing me in its warm circle of light. I drifted off knowing that when I awakened the punishment would be behind me and I'd have sense enough not to do something that stupid again.

Or so I thought.

Talking Fish

Because that year, incidents occurred like clockwork. I liked Auntie's club meetings by then, got used to the yummy dishes that were paraded into her kitchen all morning and lined up on her counters. But I'd never before seen a full-sized smoked fish waiting there. One Saturday, Miss Ida had brought over a giant smoked fish, one that looked like it should still be swimming in a lake somewhere, and set it on the table. It had an open mouth and a staring eye. Every time I looked at it, it seemed to be looking right back at me. Accusingly.

I decided to put on one of my lonely little plays outside among the sheets hanging on Auntie's clothesline. But when I went back in, that fish was still looking at me as if it thought I was up to something. Just then Auntie's fancy friend Lil came in with a pineapple. I'd never seen a real pineapple either. I stopped to watch her slice it into fat circles with the center cut out like a doughnut.

She laughed and gave me the leaf part. "Here, Junie," she said in her singsong Jamaican voice. "You can have it for a hat, don't you know." It looked just like the top of a palm tree. She laughed, squeezed my cheek, and tossed the leafy bunch in the kitchen trash.

She put the pineapple slices in a bowl and slipped it into Auntie's refrigerator "to chill," she said to me. It was another warm morning. "To chill" had such a refreshing ring.

And that pineapple made me think of Hawaii—and the hula. In fact, I began to do the hula right there in the kitchen. I hulaed out the back door and around to the front yard. There, in my pedal pushers and white tennis shoes, sockless, I hulaed with my head back, my eyes on the tall palm trees that lined Auntie's street on both sides like soldiers waving gently. I found my pop beads where I'd left them draped on the hibiscus bush and flung them around my neck like a lei. I hulaed around the yard, down the driveway, and eventually back into the kitchen, oblivious to the fish in my hula trance. I hulaed over to the refrigerator and opened the door, standing there a moment in the blast of cold air. There was that bowl of cool yellow pineapple slices. I took one off the top and stood there eating a piece while listening to the club ladies on the other side of the kitchen door.

I took another slice, then I hulaed on outside.

I made trip after trip to the refrigerator, that pineapple drew me so. I was really surprised when I reached into the bowl and found it . . . empty. I went to sit on the back steps then. I didn't feel like doing the hula anymore. I felt like hiding.

Before I knew it, Auntie was calling, "Jooooonie!" That sound went through me. The first thing I saw as I walked in the door was that big scary fish I'd forgotten all about. Its mouth gaped open as if it wanted to tell on me. I don't know why I was so scared of a dead, cooked fish, garnished with lemon and parsley and ready for eating.

My reputation was known from the pepper-cake incident, so the club ladies gathered in the kitchen behind Auntie, seemingly waiting to see if I was going to lie. Or—I thought absurdly—waiting to see if the fish was going to reveal all.

Auntie said, "Junie, do you know what happened to all that pineapple Lil brought for our meeting?"

"No, ma'am," I lied, and that lie made my face hot and my tongue seem to swell in my mouth. I started blinking fast, and some of the ladies broke into twitters behind their hands.

"Oh?" Auntie said, and I didn't like the way the "oh" started low then rose and got big.

"Ask that fish," Miss Beulah said, feeding into my fear. She looked at me slyly. "It's been in here all afternoon. I bet that fish could tell us what happened to that pineapple."

I decided right then I didn't care for Miss Beulah.

"Right now," Auntie said, "you're going to take your allowance and walk down to Yamamoto's and buy me another pineapple—which is going to cost a lot since it's just a corner grocer's. You hear me, missy?"

"Yes, ma'am."

"Go on, now," she said, frowning down at me. Her eyebrows were knit together and her mouth was pursed, but something in Auntie's eyes showed pity for me and all the forces that drove me into these predicaments. There was bewilderment there also. After all, Auntie didn't have kids. She didn't know all the ways they could act without rhyme or reason. But the remarkable thing was that in that pity and bewilderment, there was not a speck of anger. There was only a sort of scrambling after understanding.

"You know what, Imani and Blair? At one point late that afternoon, when I went into the kitchen for a glass of wa-

ter, long after the club ladies had gone and I felt it was safe to enter the house again, I heard Auntie telling my daddy that she was really worried about me. He'd spent that afternoon under the hood of Uncle Melvin's Oldsmobile changing spark plugs or something. Each time our eyes had met while I hulaed about, he'd saluted me, looking so pleased—as though all was right with the world and his children were doing okay in spite of our circumstances. That maybe he could relax and things would just work out. I felt awful that he had to hear Auntie's disturbing words. I couldn't see them, but I pictured Auntie with her hand resting on Daddy's, and him with his head bowed in disappointment, realizing nothing was as simple as he always hoped. I wished I could be as happy as Daddy needed me to be."

"Were you lonely, Mommy?" Imani asks. "Did you have anyone to play with?"

"Not a soul at first."

Red Plaid Purse

One day while I was still the bookish loner in Miss Dickerson's class, Auntie came home with a present for me. It was a red plaid purse. The front flap zipped open, and on the inside of the flap were slots for every kind of coin: half-dollars, quarters, dimes, nickels, and pennies. There was also a leather name tag on a gold chain, a little compartment for a mirror, and a loop holding a tube of pink lipstick that actually did nothing but grease your lips. The best part was that in every slot Auntie had slipped in just the right coin. I couldn't wait to take that purse to school. I'd seen a famous movie star's daughter on television standing primly beside her father with one just like it hooked over her arm.

I didn't have a best friend yet, and I thought perhaps the purse could be the doorway to a friendship with a remote girl named Ingrid. She sat on the other side of Eva, who was still trying to be my best friend. But I didn't want a fat girl like Eva for a best friend. Unless there was absolutely no one else.

Ingrid, on the other hand, was normal-sized and new like me. Except she was completely comfortable and superior-acting. I was mostly impressed by her name. Colored girls weren't named Ingrid. I imagined her being born in Germany to a GI father—coal black—and a blond mother with thick braids crisscrossing the top of her head who just said *"ja"* all the time.

Ingrid herself had two very long honey-colored braids and soft silky curls at her neck. And she was from New York, probably the suburban New York of large houses with wide, sloping lawns. Happily, Ingrid's Negro grandmother, whom she was living with for some reason I was not told, and Auntie Dot were in the same social club.

In the morning at the cloak closet, I pointed out the purse's features to Eva, but my real attention was on Ingrid and how I might be impressing her. She watched silently but with interest.

Soon a girl named Omega Brown arrived. She grinned at us, showing off a big space where she'd let a tooth rot out of her mouth. I hung up my purse, and the three of us hurried to our desks.

Everyone said Omega had cooties and had to be avoided at all costs. No one would even drink from the same water fountain she drank out of. "Omega Brown drank there!" they'd warn each other.

Later, the recess bell rang just as we were finishing our dictionary work, and we got up and filed out to play.

Halfway through jumping double Dutch, a feeling of unease washed over me. Suddenly I wanted the freeze bell to ring. That was the bell that made us halt in place while a Safety in a green armband went around collecting the balls and ropes and things.

Finally it rang and the Safeties gathered the equipment. We formed two lines, a girls' line and a boys' line, and waited for Miss Dickerson to come fetch us. It seemed like a long trek to Room 12.

As soon as we got there, I went straight to the cloak closet. We hung our jackets and placed our lunches on a shelf over the bank of hooks each morning as soon as we entered the classroom. There was my red plaid purse, its front flap hanging down, every slot empty.

Gone were my half-dollar, my quarter, my dime, my nickel, my penny, and even my name tag on its sparkling gold chain. A thick lump formed in my throat.

I marched straight to Miss Dickerson and reported the theft. Several classmates gathered around with thrilled expressions, waiting for excitement. "I'm sorry, Junie, but how will we be able to prove which nickels, dimes, and quarters are yours?"

I knew instantly she was going to be of no help, that she didn't even have the proper level of mortification. She hadn't even put down the red pencil she'd been using to correct papers.

"My name tag is gone, too."

"I'm so sorry, Junie. Perhaps it would be best if you didn't bring so much money to school in the future."

I was speechless. I went to my seat and sat there while everyone waited for me to cry. But I didn't cry. I just looked around the room wondering who had done it.

My eyes settled on Omega. She was chewing on an already bitten-down thumbnail. Omega would be just the type to steal. I sighed and turned my attention to my math book to complete that day's assignment.

Two girls in my class, Rhonda and Renee, took me on as a friend that afternoon out of sympathy (so *something* was gained by bringing in my purse) and let me walk

home with them. On the way they stopped at Yamamoto's to buy grape suckers. I had no money, of course,
so when Renee got one with a slip of paper inside the
wrapper that said *winner*, which entitled her to a free
sucker, she gave the prize to me, and life became just a
little bit sweeter.

Soon we were on the topic of what made Ingrid tick.

"I think she's mixed," Rhonda offered.

"Me, too," I said. "I been thinkin' that." I fell right into
the cool, relaxed way they spoke. It made me feel free.

"Yeah, and her mother's probably white and embarrassed she has a colored daughter," said Renee.

"Like *Imitation of Life,* only opposite," I said, and they
both looked at me, puzzled. "The movie where this
really light girl was passing for white and was ashamed
of her mother because she was a Negro."

"Yeah," Rhonda said, impressed.

"What if her mother sent her away to live with her
grandmother because she was a Negro?" Renee said.

"Naw. Her mother wouldn't have waited till she got to
fifth grade," Rhonda said with authority.

I followed Renee's lead and nodded in agreement. It
was already obvious to me Rhonda ruled.

We walked on, our minds on the mysterious Ingrid.

Later that week I learned Auntie had a treat in store for
me. Her next club meeting was going to be at Ingrid's

grandmother's, and she was taking me so that I could visit with Ingrid. I was thrilled because now I could drink in the details of Ingrid's life—put it all together and bring back what I'd learned to Rhonda and Renee.

Ingrid answered the door in pedal pushers trimmed in the same pink with black polka dots as her blouse.

"Hi, Junie," she said coolly.

"Hi, Ingrid," I said, thinking that my cotton plaid dress with plaid piping around the collar was babyish and that she was standing there thinking the same thing.

"You all be good," Auntie said as she moved past me into the living room.

"You want to go to my room?" Ingrid asked.

"Okay."

Ingrid's bedroom had a four-poster bed with a chintz bedspread that matched the tie-back curtains. She went directly to her closet and pulled down a shoe box from the shelf. "We can play with my new Ginny dolls. You don't have Ginny dolls out here, but back East everyone has one."

Apparently, there were no Ginny dolls in Chicago either. They weren't baby dolls. They were little-girl dolls with rooted hair. Rooted hair was new. Ingrid had two. One she'd dressed in red with a red tam-o'-shanter, and the other in a blue suit and tam.

She held out the one in blue to me. "Here. Red is my favorite color."

"Blue's mine," I said.

We got down on the floor and settled into serious play. I wanted the club meeting to go on forever. I was playing dolls with the mysterious Ingrid! She had pierced ears and a tiny gold ring on her finger that I knew wasn't adjustable. It was a real ring with a yellow topaz stone—probably her birthstone. She had her own little vanity and stool. She had a real wooden jewelry box on her dresser. There were pictures of lambs frolicking in a meadow over her bed. I was in awe.

"Want something to eat?" Ingrid asked.

"Okay."

She hopped up and left the room. I stayed put, not sure if she wanted me to trail behind her or not. While she was gone, I put down my doll and decided to look at her stuff. I started with her bookshelf. She had all the *Bobbsey Twins* I had. I began to count them to make sure. One was fat with something marking a place. I pulled it off the shelf. My name tag on its shiny gold chain fell to the floor. I stood staring at it for a moment. Finally, I stooped over and picked it up and slipped it in my pocket. I went back to my place on the rug, suddenly feeling *I* had done something wrong.

Ingrid came back in with a tray of little finger sandwiches and punch. We ate and drank in silence, sitting on the floor across from each other. I kept my head down, but every once in a while I snuck a peek at her calmly chewing bits of sandwich which she broke off and popped into her mouth. Her eyes were expressionless and her chin raised and slightly tilted. It was the first time I fully realized that people could be *not* as they appear, but something else entirely.

I went on playing with Ingrid, but it felt as if I was going through the motions in a kind of mechanical stupor. I said the right things, performed the necessary actions to make the Ginny dressed in blue lunch with the Ginny dressed in red, go shopping, and prepare for guests, but my heart wasn't in it. I was waiting—waiting to be released from her presence so I could make sense of what I'd discovered.

At last, Auntie was at the door telling me it was time to go. I got up without protest. If my behavior surprised Auntie, she didn't show it. I didn't look back. I didn't even look back in response to Ingrid's "Bye, Junie. See you Monday."

By Monday, Ingrid would know that I knew. And she would know that I knew she knew that I knew, and on and on—like the way two mirrors can be angled in such a way that they reflect your image over and over, never ending. I was ashamed to have wanted her for my best friend so badly just the week before. I would tell Rhonda and Renee, but not right away. One day soon I'd drop that morsel of information on them and their eyes would bug out of their heads. But for now I'd keep it to myself.

No one seemed to notice I had little to add when we'd get to speculating about Ingrid. She soon returned to New York. Mysteriously. What Rhonda and Renee really noticed was that I didn't join in with the same enthusiasm as they did when it came to cootie-calling. Sometimes I even drank from the same spigot as Omega Brown. And when I was team captain and got to choose sides for kickball, I often picked Omega, though never first—kind of as a last resort, but I picked her.

At the end of January, Omega was gone as well. It turned out she was a foster child and she'd moved on to the next foster home. Auntie refilled my red plaid purse with the money, but I put it up on the shelf in my closet after I thanked her, and from that point on I told her I was saving it. I didn't dare take it to school because I didn't want anything to happen to it. The incident had gotten me my friendship with Rhonda and Renee. Now, that wasn't necessarily an entirely good thing. They sometimes got me to do things that I didn't really want to do, but it was a small price to pay—at first—for two new best friends.

Shoe Skates

Rhonda and Renee were friends who would flank me on the way home so I didn't feel so alone, give me their winner suckers when I had no money, and advise me when I needed advice.

They both had shoe roller skates, so I wanted shoe skates, too. I wanted them desperately. Daddy said I could have a pair if I didn't get anything lower than a B on my end-of-semester report card.

"You can do it," Rhonda said as we walked home from school. The narrow gaze she shot at me almost felt like an order. Well, I was sick of strap-on metal skates and skate keys and skates slipping off in the middle of skating. Shoe skates meant freedom.

My problem was multiplication. I hadn't mastered the 6, 7, and 8 tables, and I wasn't going to, apparently. Even Miss Dickerson's threats to bar me from working on the "Early California" mural didn't inspire me to buckle down and memorize those facts.

She tested us every Friday, and every Friday I failed the test. I was a good student otherwise, and somehow I thought my straight A's in all the other subjects would pump up Miss Dickerson's general opinion of me.

Not so. She gave me a big fat D in math. It seemed to make all those A's on my progress report look tiny in comparison.

In the morning, while the class was working on the Problem of the Day in math, Miss Dickerson called me up to her desk.

"Do you understand why I gave you a D in math?" she asked.

"Yes, ma'am." I looked into those blue eyes sunk into

deep folds of fat—like twin sunrises coming over the horizon. She went on as if I hadn't answered. She had a little speech to deliver.

"I gave that D to you, June"—I frowned; I didn't like to be called June anymore—"because you earned a D or Fail on every facts quiz you've taken for the last six weeks."

"Yes, ma'am." Auntie, who was from North Carolina, would have been proud of my "ma'am"s.

"Now, if your father would like to have a conference with me . . ." My eyes must have widened a little at that suggestion, because her voice faded away for a moment. ". . . I'd be happy to arrange a time with him."

"Yes, ma'am." I backed up a little. I was ready to go.

She wasn't finished. "You're a good student, June, but you haven't been trying, have you?"

"No, ma'am, I haven't."

She smiled at my readiness to admit it. "I want you to promise me you're going to try harder from this point on."

"I promise, Miss Dickerson, from this day forward."

She grinned broadly, certain that she'd put together the right combination of words and action to bring me around—put me back on track. "You may go back to your seat now."

"Look," I said to Renee on the way home that day. "Miss Dickerson gave me a D in math."

"You mean you *earned* a D," Renee said, quoting Miss Dickerson. We both had our report cards out and she now looked at her own C in math with new respect. Rhonda wasn't showing her card and we knew not to ask.

"Let me see that," Rhonda said, snatching it out of my hand. She squinted at it. "You could make that into a B."

"No, I couldn't," I said slowly. Considering.

"Yes, you could." She cocked her head challengingly.

Renee held out her hand. "Let me see that again."

Rhonda flicked it at her as if she was dealing a playing card.

Renee scrutinized it. "You can do it," she said, falling in line with Rhonda. She handed it back to me. "You need black ink."

I had a black ballpoint in my book bag. We reached Rhonda's front walk and headed up to her porch to take care of the business of altering my progress report. With pen in hand I sat poised atop a little cliff of indecision— but only for a moment. Oh, what the heck, I thought. But just before I took the leap, Rhonda stopped me.

"Wait. Write some D's first, then practice making them into B's." If she had told me to jump off her garage roof, I probably would have.

My D's into B's looked obvious.

"That one's pretty good," Renee lied, pointing at one.

"No," Rhonda said. "You can still tell that it was a D to begin with." She held my practice sheet next to my report card.

I should have stopped right then. I should have said, "No—I can't do it." But soon I put the pen to the card and carefully traced the straight back of the D, then looped out two curves of an uppercase B.

"Looks good," Renee said quickly.

I studied it. I didn't believe her one bit, but the deed was done, so I worked on forcing myself to believe her.

"Yeah, it does," Rhonda said.

I took one last look and slipped the report card into my book bag.

That night at dinner, Junior presented his report card, unable to hold off any longer. His grades were always bad. "No TV for a month," Daddy said, and cut into his chicken breast. We were all used to Junior's underachievement. Just before Daddy took his first bite, he said, "Where's yours, Junie?"

I got up, went into my room, retrieved the card from my top bureau drawer, and returned to the table. I placed it beside his plate.

His cheeks bulged with chicken, and as he chewed and chewed he peered down at the card with a little frown.

I held my breath.

He wiped his hands on his napkin, picked up the report card, swallowed, and said, "Looks like you get those new shoe skates."

I let out my breath, a little stunned.

"I'll get them on Saturday, day after tomorrow."

Auntie smiled over at me, Uncle Melvin slapped me lightly on the back, and Junior stared into his mashed potatoes.

"You gettin' them?" Rhonda asked the next day.

"Yeah," I said. I didn't feel happy.

"You fooled him?"

I suddenly didn't like Rhonda very much. I had a vision of my father walking toward Auntie's house at the end of the day after taking the red car and two long bus rides all the way from the Long Beach Shipyard. I pictured him with his lunch pail perched on his lap, his weary eyes staring out the bus window, and I remembered how his face always broke into a smile each time he turned the corner to see me sitting on Auntie's porch waiting for him.

I thought of my daddy all day. I could hardly do my work. At lunchtime, I told Miss Dickerson I didn't feel well—which was true. She sent me to the nurse, and I got to lie on the cot with the scratchy gray blanket and paper pillow protector and stare at the tiny holes in the ceiling tiles.

"Normal," Miss Moss said, pulling a thermometer out of my mouth. "Normal as can be."

"I feel awful."

She called Auntie and got permission to send me home.

"Come in here and let me look at you," Auntie called

to me from the kitchen as soon as I walked into the house. I didn't even have to arrange my face into a pained look: I *felt* pained. She was on her stool, snapping green beans, the radio droning her noontime show. I walked over and let her feel my forehead. Auntie sighed. "You feel fine to me. But you go on in your room and lie down."

I flopped down on my bed. In desperate need of escape, I conked out immediately. Later, somewhere in my sleep I could hear everyone returning home, one after the other. Later still, I woke up to hearing their conversation at the dinner table. I feigned sleep when Daddy tapped on the door. I heard him open it, check on me, then quietly close it.

I wished I could skip over Saturday to Sunday, but Saturday came.

I woke up to the sound of cartoons on television. I strolled into the living room still in my pajamas. Only Junior seemed to be home and he was taking advantage by watching the forbidden TV.

"Where's everybody?"

"Out," he said.

I went into the kitchen to get a bowl of cornflakes and then sat down with Junior in front of *Tom and Jerry*. My munching sounds seemed as loud as the cartoons to me. Suddenly we heard Uncle Melvin's car pulling into the driveway. Junior jumped up and turned off the TV, then felt the top to see how hot it was. Daddy had been known to check the top when we were on TV punishment. Junior sucked in a deep breath and waited for them to come through the door. In my own way I felt as if I shared his guilt, so while we waited we stared at each other like co-conspirators.

Only Auntie and Uncle Melvin came in, their arms filled with bags from Sears. Daddy wasn't with them. "Your daddy wants you outside, Junie," Uncle Melvin said. He'd walked into the kitchen before I could check his face.

I went out to the porch and sat down beside my daddy. There was a big box next to him with a picture of white shoe skates on the lid. "Go on. Open it," he said.

I lifted the lid and stared down at my old pair of strap-on skates. I let my eyes meet Daddy's for just a moment, then fall back to the skates. I brimmed with shame.

"You want to explain yourself?"

"I changed the D to a B," I said, my eyes immediately tearing up. I didn't even have to force them for effect.

"That was pretty stupid, don't you think? I thought I had a smarter daughter than that."

"You did?"

"I did."

I felt my mouth droop with self-pity.

"No need to feel sorry for yourself," he said, as if reading my mind. "You can go on inside now."

I started to get up then.

"Wait a minute," Daddy said. He held up the box of old skates. "You forgot these."

I took the box out of his hands and went inside to flop on the couch. I felt bad about my deceit. But I felt worse that Daddy was disappointed in me.

I ran my hand along the shoe-skate box.

"Those your new skates?" Junior said from across the room.

"Yeah," I answered, not wanting to explain. "You better watch out—Daddy's coming to check if you've been watching TV." I said this just to be mean. Why should I be the only one suffering?

I took the box into my room and put it on a high shelf. For the next few weeks, every time I went into the closet for anything, I avoided looking up. Still—I could feel my old skates in that box staring down at me, reminding me that I was a liar and I had, once again, let down someone who'd had faith in me.

As it turned out, a month later Rhonda had her eleventh birthday. Her Grandma Nell gave her a second pair of white shoe skates with purple pom-poms. She skated over as soon as she got them. "How you like 'em, Junie?" she asked, doing a half turn.

"I like them fine."

She completed her turn. "Bet you wish you had a pair," she said, skating away, her arms pumping. She never looked back.

Imani sits up, filled with indignation. "Mommy, that's all that girl Rhonda said? Didn't she remember it was her idea that got you in all that trouble?"

"Why would she care about that?" Mommy says with a shrug. "Girls like Rhonda don't think beyond themselves too much."

Imani is quiet for a bit. "Did you ever get any shoe skates?"

"Not that year."

"Did that girl ever let you skate with hers?"

"I made sure I didn't ask her."

"Bet she wanted you to."

"I don't think Rhonda cared one way or the other."

"I don't like that girl."

Mommy smiles at Imani in the rearview mirror.

It's Not Stealing

Rhonda, Renee, and I had developed a routine after school. We stayed on the playground for thirty minutes—we had permission—intensely playing whichever game we deemed our game of the week. It would be dodgeball, tetherball, or jacks. Then we walked home down Santa Barbara so we could stop by Yamamoto's for candy. For the dime Auntie gave me each day for milk, I could buy two grape suckers or two candy bars or a Coke or a bag of chips and a candy bar. My dime went a long way.

Sometimes we went through a salty-seed stage. It was a Japanese snack—actually salted, dried plums, but we called them seeds for some reason. They had sweet ones, too, but we preferred the salty. Sometimes we bought fat dill pickles and stuck a peppermint stick down the middle so we could have two tastes going at the same time.

One afternoon, Renee and I, tired of Rhonda taking forever to make her selection and having already paid for our bags of penny candy, decided to wait outside. Soon Rhonda came bouncing out of the store and began to walk in front of us backward with a big sly grin on her face.

"What? What?" we asked in unison.

She began to laugh out loud.

"What is it?"

"Oh—something," she said. She reached around and drew out of her back pocket a packet of salty seeds.

My smile froze on my face.

"Where'd you get that?"

"In there," she said glibly.

Slowly, I looked back at the store, then at Renee, who wasn't smiling either.

"Did you steal it?"

"It wasn't stealing."

"But you didn't pay for it."

She moved out of the way and began to walk with us. "But it wasn't really stealing. It's just a game. I did it for fun."

I didn't say anything. I thought of what I'd heard about the Yamamotos. How they'd been rounded up during World War II and shipped off to an internment camp in Arizona. Auntie remembered it. She remembered how the building, with all the specials signs still on the front plate-glass window, became like a ghost store, looking sad and abandoned. But it hadn't been abandoned. One day a truck pulled up and loaded all the inventory, then boards were nailed across the door.

"I don't ever want to see the desert again, Dot," Mrs. Yamamoto once told Auntie. "I don't like heat and dust and no ocean nowhere close by. I don't even like the kind of plants that grow in the desert."

"You shouldn't take stuff out of their store," I told Rhonda quietly, almost reverently.

Rhonda sucked her teeth in disgust.

Renee said nothing.

The next day Rhonda's theft was largely forgotten—until we turned onto Santa Barbara and Yamamoto's bright green awning came into view.

"I'ma see if I can get a winner sucker," Rhonda said, dancing ahead. "I got fifteen cents. I'ma try three times.

Whatcha wanna bet that little winner slip is in the first one I buy." She looked back at us. "Come on."

Renee trotted forward. I lagged purposefully behind. "I have to tie my shoe," I said. I watched them go into the store. Soon I followed.

Mrs. Yamamoto stood at the bank of produce spraying lettuce with a little hose. Rhonda and Renee fanned out in two directions.

"Hi, Junie," she said brightly. "How's your aunt Dot?" She always asked after Auntie if she wasn't waiting on a customer. She swished the water back and forth, and my eyes darted quickly all around the store for Rhonda and Renee. I'd momentarily lost them. Rhonda was flipping through a magazine. Renee was leaning down into the open freezer for a Dreamsicle.

"Auntie's fine, Mrs. Yamamoto."

"Do you have any *Archie's Girls* comic books, Mrs. Yamamoto?" Rhonda called out. Renee moved to the shelf of penny candy: Bit-O-Honey, jawbreakers, Bazooka bubble gum, and Dubble Bubble. She picked up two packets of cherry Lik-m-Aids and slipped them into her jacket pocket. My heart began to beat fast.

"No, Rhonda, the new *Archie*s haven't come yet. Seems like we always get our magazines late." She said this as if it were some intentional injustice. She moved her hose to the bok choy. "Did you look good?"

"Uh-huh . . . ," Rhonda said slowly, and it was then

that I realized she was deliberately distracting Mrs. Ya-mamoto so Renee could take something without paying.

Renee moved to the counter. Rhonda grabbed a *Little Lotta* comic and joined her.

Mrs. Yamamoto left her produce and went to ring up their purchases. "No candy today?" she asked, and then yawned into her hand.

"No, we don't want cavities," Rhonda said.

"Smart girls."

Rhonda paid for her comic and we left the store.

"Why'd you do that?" I said, whipping around to Re-nee.

"Do what?" She hurried ahead. We caught up.

"I saw you take those Lik-m-Aids," I said.

She glanced over at Rhonda, who showed nothing on her face. Then she walked on, staring straight ahead, her lower lip poked out defiantly.

A little later she reached into her pocket, took out a Lik-m-Aid packet, and shook some of the flavored sugar into her hand. Rhonda held out her palm and Renee poured some glittering red granules into it. She held the packet out to me. "Want some?" she said, licking her top lip with her stupid red tongue.

"No. I don't want any."

"Miss Goody Two-Shoes," Rhonda said.

"I'm not Miss Goody Two-Shoes. But they're *Japanese*."

"So?"

Renee was quiet—watching.

"They had to go to an internment camp during World War II."

"So . . . I wasn't even born." She said this, emphasizing each word with a roll of the neck.

I couldn't explain what I meant, but Renee, through no intention of her own, helped me direct my feelings.

"So it'd be okay if they were white?"

I was silent, but I thought about this. It still wouldn't be okay. But—they being Japanese somehow made it worse. Bad stuff had happened to them like bad stuff had happened to us. It was worse.

My face must have shown my misery at being cornered, because Renee looked down and checked her watch. *"Bandstand!"* she cried.

"What time is it?" Rhonda said.

"Three fifty-five!" We all broke out into a run then. *American Bandstand* could not be missed. Even I, the baby of the group, loved *Bandstand*.

We burst into Rhonda's living room, snapped on the television, then hopped around while it warmed up. The screen sizzled as the picture bloomed slowly into focus. Then the *Bandstand* theme song started up (we were in time!) and we began to do the Texas hop. First Rhonda and Renee, while I danced with the front-door knob, then Renee and me. The theme song died out and we flopped down to do some serious watching and swooning over Italian guys who wouldn't give colored girls like us a thought. We didn't care that they didn't allow black people on that show. We'd just as soon relate to the girls in the blond pageboys and Capezio flats.

All things having to do with Yamamoto's were forgotten—for now.

"Come on, you guys . . . ," I said the next day as we walked home. They looked over at me innocently. "Don't take anything." We were nearing Yamamoto's, a place I now dreaded.

"I said I wasn't," Rhonda said.

She was lying.

"No, you didn't."

"Okay," she acceded, "I'm saying it now, then. Happy?"

That wasn't meant to be answered. Rhonda and Renee walked into the store blustering and animated; I hung back gloomily. It wasn't as if I was the Goody Two-Shoes they thought me to be. Of course, I knew stealing was wrong. Even if I hadn't actually been stolen from, I would know that much. But more than the obvious truth, I feared the discovery that was bound to come if they kept at it. People always got caught. Then what would Mrs. Yamamoto think of us? What would she think of Negroes?

Auntie would often say to me and Junior, "Act your age and not your color." One time she laughingly told her friends that she'd heard from Daddy that when it was first explained to Junior about us being Negro, he responded by saying, "Maybe *I* am, but I *know* Junie isn't." He was letting me out of the lodge because I was lighter and had gray eyes. We knew we had points subtracted from us from the get-go. It was our job to prove over and over to people that we weren't as bad as they assumed we must be.

So I knew the responsibility of being a Negro. You had an awful point to prove. Now, that point frightened me. It made me almost wait for Rhonda and Renee outside.

I hung back a little while longer, then walked into the store feeling as if I was following my friends off a cliff. They were at the big floor freezer, Renee leaning deep into it moving things around and Rhonda holding back the top, which was heavy and made to slide back in place as soon as it was released. I felt relief. They weren't about to stuff their pockets with drumsticks and Fudgsicles. They went up to the counter to pay. Mrs. Yamamoto, who'd been sitting behind the counter on a stool, moved her newspaper aside to make room.

Then she gave each of us a tiny frown. Her eyes came to rest on Rhonda and Renee. She didn't say anything. No usual greeting. No "Hi, Junie. How's your aunt Dot?"

Nothing. Finally she said, "I want to see what's in your pockets." Her voice was flat and resigned.

My eyes darted to Rhonda, then Renee. I saw bold indignation on Rhonda's face, fear on Renee's. I was filled with bewilderment. The times they did stuff things into their pockets, Mrs. Yamamoto didn't catch them. Now, when they hadn't done anything but bring their ice creams up to the counter to pay for them, she was mistakenly accusing. Maybe this was for the other times. Maybe she'd discovered things missing after we'd left her store on the other days, and she was assuming that we'd stolen something on this occasion.

I reached in my pockets and turned them inside out. Mrs. Yamamoto came from around the counter and pulled open my jacket. My face burned. My lips trembled. I didn't understand. I'd never so much as taken an eraser that didn't belong to me, like some kids did at school. Pencils, crayons—school supplies seemed to be fair game if they weren't nailed down.

She looked down at me as if I could have hidden some pilfered item in my hair or my shoe. She turned to Rhonda and Renee. Renee began to cry. Rhonda stood defiantly not moving. Her fearlessness unnerved me. In fact, the whole situation seemed to enliven a rebelliousness she carried around with her anyway. She was unruffled, challenging.

"Go on, girls. Let me see those pockets."

Renee, the first to crack, started pulling candy out and

placing it on the counter. My eyes bugged at the amount she'd been able to stuff in her pockets. All of us waited for Rhonda to follow suit.

She uttered a weak sort of half laugh. "I'm not turnin' my pockets inside out—because I didn't steal no candy," she said. "I didn't steal nothin'." She turned and walked calmly to the door, throwing a smirk back at the three of us over her shoulder.

Mrs. Yamamoto, small and thin and meek as a bird, let her go, but she called out, "Don't come back." I began to cry right along with Renee because that meant we were all banned. That meant I wouldn't even be allowed back to pick up a half gallon of milk or a can of coffee for Auntie. I was disgraced. I was banished. And I hadn't done anything wrong.

"You steal, Junie?" she asked me, her face heavy and sad.

"No. I never stole anything, Mrs. Yamamoto."

"But you knew they were."

That silenced me.

"I want to talk to your auntie. You come back in here—you bring your auntie with you."

"Yes, ma'am." I turned to go. I walked fast, not letting Renee catch up easily.

At the corner Rhonda was waiting, her face still arranged in righteous indignation. I kept on walking. I just wanted to get home and get my trouble over with.

"What's wrong with you?" Rhonda said at my back.

She followed us. Renee moved fast ahead of her as well. Seemingly, she didn't want anything to do with Rhonda either. Renee was going to be in more trouble than I was. She'd been caught. Her mother didn't play around. I knew Renee was already feeling the beating she had in store and the harsh sentence that would follow.

Rhonda caught up and grabbed at her arm. She ignored me. I looked back in time to see Renee pull away. "Leave me alone!" she cried. "Just leave me alone, Rhonda!" She broke into a run.

"Well, go on then," Rhonda shouted after her.

When I got home, Auntie was sitting on her stool in the kitchen ironing and smoking. Her smoldering cigarette rested in a Mason jar lid.

I dropped my book on the table and stood silent.

She took a long drag and frowned over at me. "Don't I even get a by-your-leave?"

I tried to talk but broke down crying.

"What's wrong with you?" she said. She stubbed out her cigarette and slid off her stool to come over to me and hold me by the shoulders.

I managed to hiccup out, "Mrs. Yamamoto wants to see you before I can go back into her store."

"Why?"

"She thought I was stealing, but I wasn't," I said in a rush.

Immediately, I knew Auntie believed me. I don't

know how. But she did, and I collapsed in her arms with relief.

She led me to the table and sat down across from me. In a calm voice she said, "Tell me what happened."

I told her everything, watching the changes of expression her face went through, from disbelief to pure displeasure at Rhonda's refusal to turn over her stolen candy.

"I'm calling that girl's mother."

"Auntie, she'll be mad at me for telling."

"You think I care about that? Why, if she were here, I'd paddle her little behind myself."

I liked the idea of Rhonda getting her little behind paddled.

"Junie, you made a big mistake letting this go on."

I started to protest, but she held up her hand. "Now, you listen to me. You think this is the last of this kind of situation? Girl, don't you know that something like this is going to happen over and over before you leave this world? If you don't grow some backbone, I don't know about you. You can't let people lead you down the garden path. They'll lead you right to hell."

Inwardly, I sighed, bracing myself for her garden path speech. She was always talking about people being led down the garden path if they didn't watch out.

"We gonna straighten this thing out tomorrow, first thing."

"Yes, ma'am," I said, feeling as if I'd come through a serious sickness and was now finally on the recovery side of a high fever. Auntie handed me a small paring knife then and pointed to a bowl of russet potatoes. "I need those peeled," she said. I didn't dare show the slightest displeasure. Auntie was going to take care of things, and I was too grateful to fret over having a giant bowl of potatoes to peel. Minutes later, out of the silence, Auntie said, "You be careful of those new friends of yours. They might turn out to be more trouble than they're worth."

Eventually, I was allowed back in the store after Auntie talked to Mrs. Yamamoto. Renee was allowed back in as well, but Rhonda wasn't. Renee's daddy had marched her back to the store to recite a lengthy apology and to empty out her piggy bank onto Mrs. Yamamoto's counter. But out of loyalty to Rhonda, Renee exiled herself, too. So our after-school routine didn't include Yamamoto's anymore.

Soon she and Rhonda were bad-mouthing Mrs. Yamamoto and all her merchandise, saying she charged too much and her candy was stale. Which was not true—at least the part about the candy being stale. I was always quiet during these pronouncements. Noticeably quiet. Eventually, I'd feel the weight of their judgment directed at me—Miss Goody Two-Shoes—and I'd search frantically for something to say that would divert them.

"Why were you friends with that girl?" Imani asks.

"At that age I believed certain girls had a kind of power that I wanted to be around—thinking a little crumb of it might fall my way. And then I'd no longer be as dumb and unloved and useless—and lonely." Mommy turns around and smiles at Imani. "I don't know, really. Not even now," she says mysteriously.

Mavis

I know it was Rhonda's idea—mostly—to be mean to Mavis. Mavis was a big black dog that lived in the front yard of a house we had to pass on the way to school or the public swimming pool. We decided that we didn't like her. We concocted all kinds of fantasies about her owner, ol' Mr. Broussard. He was seedy and strange and lived alone.

During those first dry, smog-scented spring days, when Saturdays filled us with the anticipation of summer, we'd pass his house and hear the drone of a Dodger game filtering out of the dark recesses of his house as if coming from a cave.

"He watches TV all day except when he has to go to the store for Wonder bread and canned peas," Rhonda said, being the most imaginative of the three of us. "Which he makes into a sandwich."

"And dog food for Mavis," Renee added.

"Mr. Broussard probably eats dog food," Rhonda said, laughing wickedly.

Then we'd drift on by, our flip-flops slapping our soles, our rolled towels pressed to our chests, pretending summer had just begun.

On the days Mr. Broussard kept his door closed and we felt safe to be mean, we'd stop and bark at Mavis—laugh while she strained futilely at her chain, barking and snarling back at us, protecting her territory. Sometimes, we'd throw soft clods of dirt at her.

"Stupid dog," Rhonda would say. "What a stupid dog."

In the split second after she'd say that, I'd feel a quick flicker of guilt and some words of Auntie's would intrude: *It's not nice to be cruel to God's creatures.* She said this the time she came upon Junior squeezing a thin line of glue around a column of ants. She must have pushed the right button, because he looked stricken and hurriedly tried to clean up the glue.

On our way back, after school, if the door was still closed, we threw more dirt and grass at her—our eyes darting back and forth between Mavis and the closed door.

Rhonda got the idea first. Hot meat. "Let's put some red pepper on some meat and give it to Mavis. See what happens."

The next morning I got the cayenne down from our spice shelf and shook some into a piece of wax paper, then folded it up and stuffed it in my jumper pocket. But suddenly I remembered the cake incident and went back to the cabinet, took down the paprika, and shook some of that into a new square of wax paper. I wasn't sure why I was doing that.

"Got the pepper?" Rhonda asked as I came down the front steps.

I handed her a packet.

She held up her sack lunch. "I got the meat."

We walked around to the side of her house, squatted in the shadow, and prepared Mavis's breakfast. I watched Rhonda sprinkle red pepper all over the top of the slice of meat loaf, her face soft with pleasure.

We cackled all the way to Mavis's yard. She barked at us warily, then stopped and stared while Rhonda lobbed the meat over the fence. It landed at Mavis's feet. Mavis gobbled it up greedily with great lapping noises while we watched, then brought her long tongue all around her chops one last time before settling down for a nap.

"She likes it," Renee whispered.

Rhonda's eyes narrowed. "Yeah . . . ," she said slowly. She gave a little shrug.

I said nothing. We walked on to school.

Our interest in Mavis took a detour when Rhonda, then Renee, got the chicken pox. "Too bad they didn't have chicken pox when they were younger," Auntie said. "It's going to be hard on them."

Now I had to walk to and from school alone. I'd leave early and take my time, stopping and staring at Mavis on her chain and feeling a little deflated when she suddenly no longer bothered to bark. What was wrong with that dog?

One afternoon, out of the blue, my feeling about Mavis changed. It was a mystery even to me. That night we had roast beef. It was my week to do the dishes. After I finished, I marched the plastic garbage holder with the big center bone out to the garbage can by the back door.

I remembered that bone as I was leaving for school the next day. I retrieved it from the garbage, wrapped it in foil, and headed to Mavis's yard. I tossed the bone over the fence, then watched Mavis pounce on it with gusto. I continued on to school feeling somehow vindicated.

I began to save a bit of lunch meat from my sandwich, and as I passed her yard, I'd toss it over the fence at her, then watch as she seemed to swallow it whole.

Mavis was becoming my secret friend. Every day I walked toward her yard with anticipation, then on to school feeling satisfied. But there was a growing problem.

Mavis was old, I discovered. In dog years. And she

was taking a sudden turn toward frailty. It was surprising when I realized it for the first time. She'd lost some of her zip—very quickly. In a few weeks' time, it seemed, Mavis wasn't rushing at us anymore.

The first time I saw Mavis get up from under the live oak and drag her hind legs behind her as she made her way heavily up her porch steps, I was filled with worry. Auntie had sent me down to Woolworth's with a swatch of ecru fabric and specific instructions to bring back thread the same color. "Don't you come in this house with white thread," she'd warned me.

With that task weighing on my mind, I watched Mavis struggle, my mouth hanging open at the sight and a wretched feeling in my heart.

"What's wrong with that dog?" Renee said the first time she noticed it. "She looks sick, don't you think, Rho?"

"She looks real sick," Rhonda said in a hushed tone. "Wonder if she's getting ready to die?"

My throat closed up. We walked on in silence, me remembering all my taunts as if someone had lined them up for me and they went all the way down the block.

"We shouldn't have been mean to her," Renee said.

"It's not nice to be cruel to God's creatures," I said, repeating Auntie's words somberly, my lips trembling. The mention of God always put us in a different place. Even Rhonda seemed fearful. We walked on quietly, each of us probably calculating how we might have to pay for our sins against Mavis. We came to Auntie Dot's walkway and I turned toward my door without looking back. "Bye," I called, dragging up the steps.

From then on, when we went by that yard we grew silent until we were safely past, our conversation momentarily frozen in reverence for Mavis's new, grave condition.

Spring break arrived and I was spending boring afternoons watering the lawn from the porch steps. I liked to aim the hose at the yellow splotches and blast the oleander bushes with their beautiful poisonous blossoms. All up and down the wide, placid avenue, bright rectangular lawns jutted out from identical two-story California bungalows, each with a tall thin palm tree standing on its own patch of curbside lawn. The phone rang behind me. Somewhere in a lazy corner of my mind I heard Auntie answer it. Then I listened to her side of the conversation.

"Mmm, mm, mm," she said. "Uh-huh—isn't that the truth."

I split the water by holding my thumb over the nozzle. I shot one stream at a big black bumblebee hovering overhead. It spiraled upward and away.

"Poor ol' Mr. Broussard," I heard Auntie say. "That poor man. That dog meant so much to him since his wife passed on."

I held my breath to hear better.

"Guess he's going to be all alone now . . . don't you know."

I dropped the hose and it whipped around like a snake for a minute, then settled down to spew water onto the driveway. I ran inside and stood waiting for Auntie to wrap it up.

"Who was that, Auntie?"

"Miss Alberta from down the street."

"What she say?"

"She can't make it to club meeting."

"No, about Mr. Broussard."

"Oh. That poor man done lost his dog. Hip dysplasia. He had to put that poor creature to sleep."

"Put it to sleep?"

"Yes. That has to be done sometimes. So a dog don't suffer."

I was horrified. Killing a dog to keep it from suffering? I went back outside and sat down on the porch. I stared at the water I was wasting. I was filled with a sinking feeling. The screen door slammed behind me.

Auntie sat down next to me. "What's the matter with you, girl?"

"Auntie, we were so mean to that dog. Now Mr. Broussard's gonna be so sad."

"Why were you mean to her?"

"I don't know. I started to be nice to her, after a while."

"That was just the good comin' out of you, Junie."

"I have good in me?"

Auntie laughed and hugged me. "You have a lot of good in you."

I studied Auntie's face. I knew she had a lot of good in her. Much more than me. And that was why I was glad she was my auntie.

I looked at everyone closely after that, passing simple and resolute judgment on them after I'd determined just how much good they had in them anyway. I considered Rhonda and Renee. Seemed to me Renee had more than Rhonda, and Rhonda didn't even think about it one way or the other. She did the most awful things without a moment's hesitation. She put spit in Renee's hair when she was cornrowing it. We were watching *Bandstand* and Rhonda said, "Renee, let me see if I can French-braid your hair." (We called it French-braiding then.) Renee, on the floor, backed up to where Rhonda was sitting on the couch. Rhonda had the rattail comb poised and waiting.

She released Renee's long wavy hair from its ponytail and drew a fine part down the middle. She started on one side. I pulled my eyes away from the TV screen and Rhonda smiled at me secretively, then pushed her lips out like a fish to form a silent "Sshh . . ." She licked her hand and smoothed down the frizzy surface of Renee's hair.

I frowned. Hadn't Rhonda wanted to comb my own

hair the day before? I turned away, fixed my eyes on the screen, lost myself in the cheering and swooning over a singer who had absolutely no talent. But he had Elvis's hair and crooked smile. Or maybe he was forcing his mouth to go up on one side. I didn't want to be in on Rhonda's sneakiness. Maybe that was the pinch of good in me.

"But you didn't tell Renee," Imani says, watching her mother's profile.

"I said 'pinch of good' . . . just a pinch."

"I wouldn't have been friends with that girl. She was awful."

"And she got me to be awful to Eva. Remember her? I mentioned her earlier."

"The fat girl."

We're Not Liking Eva

"We're not liking Eva today," Rhonda said one rainy spring morning as we huddled under a single umbrella on our way to school.

"Why?" I asked, taken off guard. I shot a glance at Renee. She didn't seem surprised. They'd obviously discussed it before they picked me up. Now Renee's eyes skirted the treetops, as if to divorce herself from this part of it—informing me.

"Because," Rhonda answered.

"For how long?"

"Till I say. What's wrong?" she asked suspiciously.

"Nothing." But a lot was wrong. My heart was growing heavier and heavier with dread. I pushed the feeling away and walked on silently.

As soon as we entered Room 12, we headed for the cloak closet to hang up our raincoats. I unbuckled and slipped out of the ridiculous rubber shoe covers Auntie made me wear.

"I sharpened your pencil for you," Eva said to me immediately after I sat down.

"Thanks," I said in a voice that was so low, I barely heard it myself.

I stared at the Problem of the Day, pretending to be lost in concentration. Following suit, Eva yanked a piece of notebook paper out of her three-ring binder and began to stare at the problem herself. She was better than me in math, and soon she was scribbling away, stopping every once in a while to wiggle her pencil between her thumb and forefinger and squint at the board.

Actually, I wasn't that interested in the Problem of the Day. I was only pretending so I wouldn't have to talk to her.

Rhonda's plan didn't reveal itself until lunchtime, when we all sat with our desks cleared, hands folded, and mouths zipped to prove to Miss Dickerson we were ready to line up for the cafeteria. Rhonda rummaged through her book bag. Miss Dickerson looked at her, waiting—probably anxious to get to her own tuna sandwich and iced tea in the teacher's lounge. Finally Rhonda sat up and folded her hands.

As soon as we were in the hall, we had to stop to let the kindergartners from early lunch go by. Rhonda handed me a small white envelope. Susan Kamei turned around. Rhonda put one in her hand. She gave one to Renee, passed one up to Linda Moreno, Pat Troy, and Sandra Buckner. She gave a small white envelope to almost every girl in line, skipping over Eva several times to get to the next chosen girl. We watched, perplexed. Eva watched, her eyes wide and bright with expectation, one hand slightly raised to receive her small white envelope as well. It was only when Rhonda had distributed every one that Eva slowly brought her hand down to her side.

Feeling her disappointment and embarrassment, I slipped mine in my pocket. As soon as Miss Dickerson dropped us at the lunch area, where some of us turned toward the cafeteria line and the rest dashed to established spots among the long blistered tables and benches, we dropped our lunches and tore open our sealed white envelopes, already surmising we had invitations. Invitations to what—we were dying to know.

· · · · ·

What: Rhonda's Super Slumber Party
For: Just becuz
When: Saturday May 10th
Where: At Rhonda's of course
Be there or be square!

It became clear what Rhonda meant by "super," because as we talked around our tuna fish or peanut butter and jelly or cold grilled cheese, she was winding through the tables and benches distributing white envelopes here and there to girls in the other fifth-grade class.

I peeked over at Eva, who sat at the end of the bench a little away from the rest of us. Her head was bent over her container of pudding. Of all of us, she had the best lunches: the crusts were cut off her sandwiches and her carrot sticks were uniformly julienned. A strange wave of something that almost felt like fear washed over me. I wasn't sure what it was or why it was there. But while excitement grew around the table with plans of what pajamas to wear and what 45's to bring, I began to feel more and more set apart, strangely more aligned with Eva, the left-out girl, than the invited girls. I must have known even then that being included was a fickle thing. Any small misstep could put a person in Eva's boat. My feelings irritated me, but Eva irritated me more. Why was there always someone like her in every class who seemed to beg for people to be mean? It was her own stupid fault, I decided, that she wasn't invited. And if she didn't lose weight and start wearing more up-to-date clothes instead of those cotton dresses with piping and sashes and buttons down the back (that I'd just gotten away from myself), if she didn't stop bringing careful little lunches and her school supplies in a neat zippered pouch with her name embroidered across the top—she would never be included in anything. I sneaked another look. She was eating her pudding with a white plastic spoon. That right there was too perfect. She should have brought a metal one from home. She should have had to hear from her mother or her grandmother or her auntie, "Girl, you better bring my good spoon back home if you know what's good for you."

Like the rest of us.

Dropped

Isn't it funny how you can know something but keep it at bay—even from your own self? That sense of dread I'd felt around Eva's situation must have been my certain knowledge that I was going to be next. Rhonda was going to decide I needed to be traded in for someone better, like Brenda Graham. From the other fifth grade. She was pretty and smart and she was on toe in ballet class, while Rhonda, who'd just started taking lessons, was still trying to make her feet do the five positions correctly. She wasn't about to drop Renee. They'd been friends since kindergarten and Renee was loyal, more loyal than Rhonda sensed I was.

When I think back on it, it seems my rejection began the Monday we were making get-well cards for a girl in our class who was in the hospital with asthma. I was happily coloring the hearts on my card bright red. I got up to ask Miss Dickerson if I could go to the bathroom. She said it was too close to lunch and she was sure a big girl like me could wait.

When I returned to the table, Rhonda had my red crayon.

"I was using that," I said to her.

"So? Now I'm using it," she answered.

"And I got dibs after Rho," Renee said without looking at me.

"That's not fair."

"It is, too, fair. I thought you were finished with it," said Rhonda.

"I went to ask to use the rest room."

"Well, you shouldn't have put it down."

I looked at my card. I could work on the flowers on the border. I picked up a blue crayon and began to color my bluebells. Soon Rhonda passed the red crayon behind my back to Renee. I looked down the long table at the crayons in other cups. Not one red crayon available.

"Let me have it when you're finished, Renee," Rhonda

said. "I still need it." I peeked over at Rhonda's card. It was an exact duplicate of mine. After a few rounds of this passing the crayon back and forth behind my back, a red one became available at the end of the long art table.

When my card was finished, I carefully printed a message inside, put it in the tray on Miss Dickerson's desk, and returned to my seat to read and wait anxiously for the bell so I could get to the rest room. As soon as Renee took her seat across from me, she asked, "What's wrong, Junie?"

"Nothing." I kept my eyes on my book.

"You mad?"

"I'm not mad."

"You seem mad." For a brief moment, our eyes met and I sensed something like discomfort in Renee. She got up then and returned to the art table to finish her card and whisper with Rhonda.

Over the next week I began to have an itchy fear—beneath the surface—as their treatment of me ran hot and cold. We'd be sitting on the grass at lunch and they'd start passing secrets back and forth while I looked on. Or as we walked home they'd simultaneously break into their special crazy-leg walk. But then as soon as I joined in, they'd stop as if they'd suddenly lost interest.

Worse were the times I'd make a comment to Rhonda

or ask her a question and she would let a few beats go by before responding. In those few seconds, while she fixed me with her blank stare, I'd die a little.

One Friday, just before lunch, while we did our "sustained silent reading," I saw Miss Dickerson nod briefly in the direction of Rhonda, and Rhonda and Renee simultaneously rose from their seats, went to the cloak closet for their matching sweaters (they'd begun dressing alike), and left the room. I stared after them. On Fridays kids could go home for lunch if they brought a note. They'd planned this—without me.

Eva joined me on the lawn at lunch with her stupid, eager chatter. At one point all I wanted to do was scream, "Shut up!" If I had to be miserable I should at least be able to be miserable in peace.

Why were they doing this to me? More important, just how long did they plan to keep this up?

After lunch, Rhonda and Renee bounced through the door, seconds after we'd all taken our seats. Timed, I suspected, to make an entrance.

"How come you didn't go to lunch with Rhonda and Renee?" Eva whispered.

"None of your beeswax. And stay out of my business," I answered, hoping it had stung enough to shut her up.

The rest of the afternoon, Rhonda and Renee behaved as if nothing was out of the ordinary. We worked on our papier-mâché replicas of the seven continents. Rhonda,

Renee, and I were in the group doing Antarctica. Miss Dickerson was going to put the continents on a big mural and display it in the glass case next to the attendance office as testament to our many hands-on learning experiences.

Out of nowhere, Renee lobbed a wad of wet newspaper at me. She laughed and checked to see if Miss Dickerson had noticed. During the split second I was deciding if this was a good or bad thing, Rhonda launched a spoonful of paste at Renee. I fell into it filled with relief. We were still friends. So what if they went to lunch without me. It was probably something arranged by their mothers anyway. I pitched a bit of wet newspaper at Rhonda and she returned with a clump of her own. We grew so tickled with our secret game, Miss Dickerson looked over at us to see what was going on.

We walked our crazy-leg walk almost all the way home. "See you," they said in unison as I skipped up Auntie's front steps. The storm had passed.

But on Monday they missed picking me up. I waited in front of the screen door until the last minute, hoping to see them turning the corner. Finally I walked to school alone.

"What happened to you guys?" I said, marching right up to where they stood with some girls from Miss Miller's class. A silence descended—on everyone. Rhonda spoke up first. "We had to get here early."

"Oh," I said, and saw exchanged looks all around.

Of course Eva filled me in later. "They have a cheer-leading team," she half whispered with self-importance. "Didn't they ask you to join?"

"Who's on it?" I said, ignoring her question.

"Some of the girls in Miss Miller's class. They're the ones who started it. They asked Rhonda to join and she told them only if Renee could—so that's how she got to be on it. They didn't ask you?"

Her eyes were big and round and excited. And she'd said all this in one exhaled breath. It was certainly clear to me why no one liked Eva. It wasn't just because she was fat. There was something else. I couldn't put my finger on it but I was sure of its existence. I turned away and busied myself in my book bag. I'd had enough of her.

I looked for clues all day that they were on the verge of asking me to join. They had to. When neither one mentioned it, I forced the issue. As everyone packed up to go home, I said as offhandedly as I could, "You guys wanna come to my house to watch *Bandstand*?"

"Can't," Rhonda said. "We're on this cheerleading team and we have practice." She snapped her book bag shut and swung it over her shoulder. "Renee," she said, leaning to the side to see around me. "Come on, let's go."

I was stunned, unable to move. I closed my mouth, which I realized had dropped open. A lump formed in my throat. I felt my face growing warm and I knew it was turning red, a characteristic I hated. I'd been teased about it often enough. "Look at Junie, she's blushing . . ."

At my side I discovered Eva, slowly and deliberately slipping her speller into her book bag, carefully zipping it closed, flush with stealthy observation. My own speller wouldn't go into my book bag. I had to empty it out and repack it before I could get everything to fit. All the time I felt Eva watching and judging me.

"See you," I said, disappointing her with my fake calm. Could I get home before I began to cry? Could I make it?

I walked home quickly, my chin aimed at my chest. I didn't care about how defeated I looked. I just wanted to be somewhere where no one could see me. I heard quick steps behind me. I looked over my shoulder and saw Eva hurrying to catch up with me. I turned back around and walked faster. She caught up.

"You want me to walk with you?" She could barely wheeze that out.

I was suddenly filled with fury. "No! No! No!" I shouted as I hurried away. "And don't you ever ask me that again!" I didn't look back but I imagined her frozen in place for the whole time it took me to get to the end of the block and turn the corner. I didn't regret it even weeks later when Miss Dickerson called an emergency meeting to talk about how important it was to be kind to everybody. She'd heard that some students in Room 12 were ostracizing one of their classmates. It had been brought to her attention by that child's mother, and Miss Dickerson was simply mortified that students in her class could be so mean.

She was going out of her way not to mention gender. But we all knew it was Eva she was talking about, because she'd prudently sent Eva to the first grade to tutor some of Mrs. Cunningham's slower learners.

That afternoon Eva had sat at the outdoor lunch table alone, reading while breathing through her mouth. Occasionally she would push her glasses back onto the bridge of her nose with her middle finger, the other fingers stiffly fanned out.

"Look at Eva," Rhonda had said with a half snort, half laugh. She said it in a tone in which I hoped she'd never say my name. Poor Eva, innocently munching one of her julienned carrots, seemed unaware of the fact that she was being summed up and that everything wrong about her simply went without saying. I didn't want to be Eva—but that was where I was headed.

Rhonda and Renee began to talk about things they'd done without me. They began to spend the whole way to school refreshing each other's memory about the details of all their fun that left me out. Laughing and rolling their eyes and jumping around with excitement at the memory of who they saw at the movies and what they ate. I struggled to pretend disinterest.

I went to Auntie for advice.

"Have you done something to them girls?"

"No," I said. "I didn't do anything to them. They're being mean for fun."

"Well, maybe you can invite one over to play and not the other, get to the bottom of it."

I thought about this. Did Auntie really know what she was talking about?

"It seems to me those girls kind of feed off each other," Auntie mused. "It might be just the thing to separate them. Invite one over for Saturday." And because we'd been suffering through a heat wave, she added, "I'll let you make ice cream."

Happily, something occurred that paved the way for this to be possible. At the movies on Sunday (I learned this later since I wasn't there) Rhonda bit down on a jawbreaker and broke a tooth that had been weakened by a cavity. She had to leave early on Monday to go to the dentist.

That afternoon during dictionary work, I passed a note up to Renee:

Renee,
Can you come over Saturday? Auntie's letting me make ice cream.
Junie

I watched my note get passed along until it finally reached its destination. Renee opened it. She read it. It took her a long time, it seemed to me. Finally, she looked back, kind of shrugged, and mouthed, "Okay." I was ecstatic.

Saturday morning, Renee walked over. True to her word Auntie was letting us make peach ice cream from some peaches she'd canned the previous summer. Before we even started we sat at the table hunting through Auntie's cookbook for a cake to go with it. I began to make light talk, trusting that I would know the moment when it would be safe to probe.

The radio played "You Talk Too Much" behind us and we sang right along. Renee was being her old self— funny and friendly. We decided we didn't want to go through the trouble of measuring dry ingredients and greasing and flouring cake pans after all. Auntie walked us through the peach-ice-cream-making process, and finally we went out to the back porch to sit on the steps and turn the crank.

"This is fun, huh?" I said, wondering if she found it as much fun as doing things with Rhonda.

I waited for her answer.

"Uh-huh," she finally said, much to my relief. My mind raced to the next activity we could do together. "Want to ride bikes later?" I asked.

"I didn't bring my bike."

"I could ride you home on my handlebars."

"My mother doesn't like me to ride on handlebars."

"I can walk you home to get it."

"I don't know . . ." She turned away from me and fixed her gaze on Junior shooting baskets in the hoop Daddy had mounted over the garage. "Why can't we just stay here?"

I turned the crank and followed her line of vision.

Finally Auntie came out to check the ice cream and told us that it was ready to go into her big freezer on the back porch. She ceremoniously moved things to make room for it and closed the lid. *Shwump.* Now we had to wait. Renee looked bored.

"Maybe I'll come back."

"Want to play Monopoly?" I suggested.

She squinted. "Not really. How long will it take for the ice cream to be ready?" she asked.

I looked at Auntie.

"Why, baby?" Auntie asked. "You got a job to get to?" Auntie allowed herself a flicker of a smile to show that she was teasing, but I felt the challenge in Auntie's question, her displeasure in Renee's veiled rudeness to me.

"No, I just have to get home pretty soon."

"Well," Auntie said, "you could come back another day."

I could see Renee weighing the possibility of the ice cream being eaten up before she could get back for it.

"No, that's okay," she said. "I guess I can wait."

"You sure, now?" Auntie said.

Renee nodded, then waited for me to say something.

"Let's go to my room," I said.

"Okay."

With the "okay" there was a little shrug. I felt desperate.

However, after about twenty minutes of Monopoly, we got into the game. She seemed to be enjoying herself. Then Junior, passing my door, poked his head in. "Can I play?" he asked.

"We're already playing," I said.

"Just start a new game," he suggested.

And that's when I noticed something.

The look on Renee's face clearly changed. Something new was there when Junior walked into the room. Lately, he'd added a little swagger to his step. Now he patrolled the game board with his cocky walk, assessing our progress and being friendly, personable—even polite to me, speaking in a suave, measured way. For the first time, Renee seemed wholeheartedly happy to be there—at my house, in the game, in my company. She turned giggly and silly and eager to upset my game while I was winning and start all over to accommodate Junior. But I wasn't having it. Oh, no, not when I had just gotten Park Place and was zeroing in on Boardwalk. Not when she had been so lukewarm all afternoon.

"No," I said, throwing the dice. "We're in the middle of a game and I'm winning. You'll just have to play another time."

"Come on, Junie," he begged. "Come on . . ."

"I don't mind. Junior can play," Renee said. "I really don't mind starting over."

"You don't mind 'cause I'm winning."

"Dang, Junie, I don't know why you have to be like that. Let your brother in the game. Come on. He wants to play."

"What's it to you?" I said.

"Ex*cuse* me?" she said, rolling her neck.

"You're excused," I said coolly.

Junior watched us, smirking. He loved drama.

"Why you care so much about Junior?" I said, feeling bold. "It's not like you're such an oh-so-nice person. You haven't been nice to *me*."

"What?"

"You and Rhonda. You've been all in your own little club."

"What are you talking about?" she asked, shooting a look at Junior to check how he was taking this.

"You guys have been going places without me, joining cheerleading and stuff, going shopping and to movies and not even asking me to go . . ."

"So, what of it? What's wrong with going to the movies by ourselves? Maybe we wanted to see something that you wouldn't want to see."

"What would I not want to see that you'd want to see?"

She rolled her eyes. "Rhonda and I like the same

clothes. And you probably don't like what we like. Plus, what *you* like *we* wouldn't like."

That didn't even make sense. It was an insult, like they were such *teenagers* and I was still a baby. They had jumped some grown-up hurdle that I hadn't.

It suddenly dawned on me why I had been demoted. They didn't think I was really like them. I wasn't, I knew deep in my heart, but it was something I'd avoided admitting.

I stood up. It was a gesture that meant the game was over, and it was time for Renee to leave my house whether the ice cream was ready or not.

She stood up. I'd let her see herself out. Junior, who'd taken a comfortable seat on my bed, sat with his chin resting on the palm of his hand, his knees apart, elbow propped on a knee. He looked amused. "Guess you ain't friends with her no more."

"So—I don't care."

We listened to the front door shut.

"Bet you do."

"She only wanted you in the game because she likes you."

He chuckled at this. A low, almost silent, old man chuckle.

"Do you like her?" I ventured.

He shook his head, turning his mouth down in a distasteful way.

I was silent. It would be just like my brother to feel like a big man around a fifth-grader and bask in the adoration. I sighed. I needed to think about more important things because now it was going to be war, with me against the world. Rhonda and Renee were popular. Everyone was going to side with them. I was going to be demoted all the way down past Eva to Omega Brown.

At least when Monday morning rolled around, I had the good sense to skip down my front steps without waiting. For the first half block I actually felt brave, but with each step taking me closer and closer to Bella Vista Elementary with its broken-pottery roof, my spirits began to sag. I passed through the gate in the tall chain-link fence surrounding the schoolyard and looked around.

There was Rhonda, standing in the midst of a group of fifth- and sixth-grade girls. I stopped in my tracks just at the moment she swung around and caught sight of me. "Jooonie . . . ," she called. She turned away from her group, facing me squarely, her body slightly bent, arms pressed to her sides, head forward. With enthusiasm, not anger. "Come over here!"

I approached slowly, carefully.

"Look what I got," she said, smiling slyly. Out of her jacket pocket, she pulled a grape sucker. "Here." She handed it to me. "I got me another one." She was grinning at me with the sun in her eyes, which made her squint, giving her face a positively diabolical look. I took the sucker out of her hand with sudden and complete understanding. I had a cute (cute to a fifth-grader) older brother named Junior, who'd shown Renee (in her own mind) some attention, which Renee had reported to her good friend, Rhonda. Rhonda wasn't about to be outdone by Renee. It wasn't the natural order of things.

I was being granted a reprieve. I could breathe a sigh of relief. In fact, I would be surprised if things didn't just slide back to normal. I slipped the sucker into my pocket. I wasn't about to pass up a good thing.

Imani sits quietly, thinking. Blair is back to sleeping with his thumb in his mouth. Every minute or so he gives it a few tired sucks.

"*You let that girl treat you like that?" Imani says after a while.*

"*Yes. I did.*"

"*I wouldn't have.*"

"*So you think. God only knows.*"

The car is moving slower now. They are at the part of the trip where they've left the Grapevine and are now pulling up the winding mountain road. Imani doesn't like this part of the trip, having to peer down into the deep ravine on her side of the car. She should have sat on the other side. But it was the hot side when they'd started out. "Tell me about when your mother finally came," she says to take her mind off the drop.

"Oh yes. Well, it was just like that—after not seeing her for nine months."

Just Like That

She was coming. It was June and just like that she was coming out to Los Angeles to see how she'd like it. As soon as I found out, I began to inspect Los Angeles as if I was seeing it through my mother's born-and-bred Chicago, Illinois, eyes. Measuring and weighing everything I felt might fall short to her: no seasons at all, no sense of fashion—everyone dressed so much more casually because of the warm weather. No really good winter coats—not that anyone ever needed one. But my mother had always had a whole wardrobe of coats and was proud of it.

There had been whispered conversations on the telephone with Daddy.

"Hurry up. Your daddy and mommy need to talk," Auntie would tell me and Junior when Mommy called, and we pumped her with the same questions we'd asked for months: "When you comin'? Have you seen Aja? What'd she say? Is it snowing yet? Is it getting warm yet?"

Lately the phone conversations were pared down to

just a short exchange of polite inquiries that served as sort of an introduction to Daddy's time with her. He'd take the receiver out of our hands and go off with it to the deserted dining-room table and sit there in the dark, not bothering to turn on the light.

"Are you excited?" Renee asked. I was still sort of friends with her—when Rhonda wasn't around—but my relationship with Rhonda had cooled for good. She was trouble, and I was outgrowing my need for her kind of "friendship."

"Kinda," I said. Truth was, I was both excited and not excited. I was confused about how I felt. I suppose deep down inside I was happy, but on the surface I felt as if I'd been shelved and now I was being taken down and dusted off.

"What do you think of my mother coming, Auntie?" I asked her while she rolled out dough for a pie. I was peeling Granny Smith apples. I salted a green sliver of peel and popped it into my mouth.

"I think it's wonderful." I couldn't really see her face, because her head was bent over her rolling, but she asked, "How do you feel?"

"Fine," I said slowly, and she looked up.

"You don't sound fine. Why's that, you suppose?"

"I dunno."

"Are you scared?"

"What if she doesn't like me anymore?"

Auntie came around the table and gave me a big hug. "Why wouldn't she like you, Junie?"

"Why did she let us go, then?"

"Honey, just because she's your mother doesn't mean she can't have problems that seem bigger than what she could handle."

I kept peeling and thought about that, realizing I didn't quite know what Auntie meant.

"Will she stay, Auntie?"

"I think she will."

"Will she like it here?" I looked past her through the kitchen window. The Helms Bakery truck was pulling up across the street. Our day was Saturday for the Helms truck. When I had money, I'd run to stand on the curb at the sound of its horn and wait for it to pull up in front of me. Then I'd step into the truck to inspect the drawers of doughnuts and cinnamon buns and cupcakes, bread and rolls, trying to decide what my dime should buy. Maybe my mother would appreciate having a bakery pull right up to her door once a week.

Daddy invited us out to the porch after dinner to talk. To tell us all the ways we could make Mommy happy if we really tried. Make her want to stay and be with us. I looked up at the waxing strawberry moon, my moon, and wondered what we had done to make her not want to be with us.

"When's she coming?" Junior asked quietly. I guess he

wanted to know when his good behavior would have to officially begin since it had been so poor all year long. When he would have to turn over that new leaf he was always promising to turn over. Junior had been turning over new leaves all his life.

"In a couple of weeks. I'll let you know for sure."

I didn't care for that answer. I picked at a callus at the base of my ring finger. I'd gotten calluses all the way across both hands from swinging on the rings at school. I was nearly as good as Rhonda, having worked up to fifty-three circuits without hopping off.

"What do you think, Junie?" Daddy asked me.

"I think it's fine."

"How come she didn't come before now?" Junior asked.

"She's coming now," Daddy said. "Let's be happy about that."

We sat quietly for a little while longer, then Daddy went inside to read the paper and watch Ed Sullivan on television. Uncle Melvin loved that show. He loved the singing and dancing and funny skits. Junior could do a good Ed Sullivan imitation—hunching his shoulders and filling his mouth with air and drawing his lips down like a monkey, but he had to be careful not to do this near Uncle Melvin. He wouldn't have found it funny one little bit. Ed Sullivan was his hero.

I looked through the big picture window at Daddy in

his chair with the paper folded open in front of his face and wondered what behavior changes *he* would have to make. As far as I knew, my daddy was perfect. My mother must have been the most difficult person in the world not to be happy with my daddy.

The date of her arrival would fall on a Monday, so the preceding Saturday Auntie skipped her club meeting, and she and I took the number 42 bus up Santa Barbara to Western, then the 25 down Western where Lou's Beauty Salon was located. Once a week, Auntie came home from this establishment with her hair sculpted into a do that had to be maintained with hairnets and clippies and spray. "Not too long ago colored folks didn't live west of Central," Auntie said, leaning over to whisper in my ear.

"How come?" I asked.

"Because we weren't allowed."

"I would have moved where I wanted anyway," I said. And at the time it seemed I'd never said a truer thing.

Auntie laughed at that. A great big belly laugh until some of the riders looked back to stare. "Junie, Junie, Junie," she said when she caught her breath. Then she stood up to pull the cord. Our stop had come.

I'd never been to a beauty parlor before, and I soon learned it was the most interesting place on earth. The first thing I noticed was the continuous swirl of grown-up conversation all around. Gossip galore. And I couldn't even be sent out of the room! I was bolted there by the attention that was going to be paid to my long bushy mane: the washing of it, the rinsing of it, the nearly arm-breaking combing of it . . . Then under the dryer to be temporarily cut off from all the juicy talk.

Miss Lou wandered over every once in a while to reach under the big steel hood, feel my hair, and announce, "Not dry yet. Just a little while longer, baby."

Later, after I'd been under the dryer for what felt like hours, just as my ears began to burn, Miss Lou declared my hair dry enough to move on to the next phase. Hot-combing it.

"Louise, you got a job ahead of you, don't you know," one lady said as she checked the progress of her own skimpy hair in the long bank of mirrors.

I sat in the swivel chair while Miss Lou draped me with a small sheet and clipped all my hair to the top of my head, leaving one small square loose at the neck. Then she began.

"Hold your head down, baby, all the way." I liked the easy way she called me baby. Living without a mother made me soak up any amount of affection with desperation.

I obeyed.

After an hour or so, she'd straightened every strand. While she assembled the next set of tools to use on my hair, I leaned forward and looked over my shoulder into the mirror so I could check the progress. My hair was nice and long. I couldn't wait to go to school and show it off.

But then she began to hot-curl it until I wound up with a head full of corkscrews. She sent me over to a chair in the waiting area to look at an old *Sepia* or *Ebony* or *Jet* magazine while the curls cooled and set.

"Her mother's coming Monday," I heard Auntie whisper to Miss Lou, her voice a stage whisper in the sudden quiet. My stomach jumped and it took minutes before I could calm down enough to pretend concentration on the recipes in *Ebony*'s monthly feature called "Date with a Dish."

"Now, you have to be very careful for the rest of the day and all day tomorrow not to sweat your hair out," Auntie said as we boarded the bus for home. "No running around—no playing rough."

I nodded solemnly. I hadn't planned on running around, but Auntie's reminder sobered me even more.

The rest of Saturday and all day Sunday I felt as if I was walking around with a telephone book on my head. I did everything in slow motion. Auntie loosely tied a scarf over my hair to protect it from the hot clouds of steam while I washed dishes, and Sunday night she rolled it in rags so that the curls would stay. She debated out loud as to whether I should be kept home from school the next day, but she decided that I should go.

Daddy, who was taking the day off—I guess to work on his nerves—borrowed Uncle Melvin's car and drove me and Junior to school. We got there after the second bell rang (Daddy had taken such a long time dressing), so I got to make an entrance with my new hair. All eyes followed me to my seat. I eased into my chair and waited for my name as Miss Dickerson went through the roll. "I got my hair done because my mother is coming tonight," I whispered to Eva.

She breathed loudly through her mouth as her eyes swept over my hair. Her hair was gathered into a small ponytail. Soon the pressure of staring eyes lessened, and we all got down to the work of solving the Problem of the Day.

During recess, I sat on the bench and read. At one point I noticed Rhonda and Renee looking at me. I didn't care. Rhonda could say "Look at Junie" in that voice she reserved for Eva all she wanted. I had more important things on my mind. Nothing outside of the knowledge that my mother was coming could touch me. I was in tune only to that huge fact.

The day wore on and finally we'd reached the last period. "June, help pass out the dictionaries," said Miss Dickerson. It was the final week of school, but there were new spelling words written on the board anyway.

I hated dictionary work. I never knew which definition to pick when there was more than one, and Miss Dickerson, using this tedious, quiet activity to give her time to correct papers and plan lessons, hated to be disturbed. If we dared ask her which definition she wanted, she'd raise her head from her work, squint her eyes, and a crease would grow across her forehead. Then she would look at you for a few seconds before answering, as if she was storing your interruption in her memory bank and was going to come up with a way to make you pay later.

I'd just finished passing out the dictionaries and had settled down to attack the first word when the door opened and someone peeked in. She must have pointed at me, or maybe Miss Dickerson had been informed beforehand, but suddenly as I was rummaging around in my pencil case, I heard "June."

I looked up and into my mother's face.

Her newly short hair curled around her face, and she looked smaller than I remembered. Who was this strange woman in clothes I'd never seen before with that curlicue haircut? A style I felt betrayed by, as if she should have consulted me before cutting all her hair off. She stayed in the doorway, and it was Miss Dickerson who broke the silence. "June, your mother's here to take you home early." She rose out of her seat and walked over to introduce herself. My mother seemed to shrink with a shyness I'd never seen in her. She smiled into my teacher's face, took a quick peek at me, and I saw a tremble in the hand she was extending to Miss Dickerson.

"Is that your mother?" Renee whispered to me.

I nodded. It was all I could do.

"She's pretty," Eva said. "She looks Mexican."

I studied my mother closely. She looked to me like the movie star Dorothy Dandridge. I hadn't gotten my mother's good looks. I was what they called rhiny: yellowish coloring and sandy hair, and I had gray eyes with lashes so pale they looked nonexistent. Junior called me Baby Paste Face when he wanted to be especially mean. Then Auntie would come back with "People don't make themselves," which didn't help me feel all that better.

I stood up, and before I knew it, with no thought of my classmates, I walked right into my mother's arms and began to cry.

"Hi, Mommy," I said. She gave me a squeeze, then released me. We moved through the door arm in arm.

After we collected Junior, we walked quietly all the way to the car—a silence that felt entirely appropriate. Mommy was driving Uncle Melvin's car, and Junior rode in the front and me in the back. I kept my eyes fixed on the back of Mommy's head. Now she seemed perfectly poised and confident in her cream sweater set with brown-and-orange scarf knotted around her neck. Every once in a while our eyes met in the rearview mirror and she winked at me. I didn't wink back. What was Junior thinking up there in the front seat sitting next to our mother? I couldn't tell by the set of his shoulders. He seemed to be sitting at attention.

I thought about nothing much at all. Just let my mind wander from Ingrid to Omega to Yamamoto's corner grocery store. My eyes felt heavy and I realized I was coming down with something. Before I knew it, we were pulling up in front of Auntie's and all the unknowns were poised to begin.

They pull off the freeway and soon they're on the dark streets that lead to Auntie's. The story of how Mommy's mother came just like that always leaves Imani a little sad and feeling sorry for her own mother. She studies her now, trying to detect some long-ago sorrow. Mommy calmly turns the wheel, and they're easing down the streets that take them to Auntie's house. Always it looks the same to Imani. Deserted and still—not the same streets she imagines in Mommy's stories. Yamamoto's is no more. It has been razed, and now a mini-mart with squeezed parking and only one way in and one way out has sprouted in its place. Mrs. Yamamoto is still alive but has long since moved to the Arizona desert to be near her grandchildren. Mommy is right. People never really do know what they are going to do. Life is too full of unexpected twists and turns.

Finally they turn down Browning Avenue. Strange. There is no porch light on at 4826. Imani and her mother look at each other, Imani sensing her mother's quiet alarm. Auntie always has the porch light on when they are expected. What's going on? Is Auntie at home? She's always at home when they are expected. They would be coming up the walkway and see her yank aside the door curtain and peek out. Then she'd throw the door open and stretch out her arms. After a long monotonous journey, the golden light behind her would be a welcome sight. And the aroma of fresh-baked Sock-It-to-Me cake warm from the oven. That scent and the mention of homemade peach ice cream would make their mouths water even if their stomachs were still a bit full of the fast-food tacos they'd eaten not long before.

Mommy pulls up in front of Auntie's slowly, the car almost creeping to a stop. Imani still feels the tiny itch of her mother's fear. The three of them say nothing.

"Maybe Auntie is at Miss Ida's," Imani says, answering Mommy's unspoken question.

"Honey, Miss Ida passed on last year, right after Uncle Melvin passed. Don't you remember me telling you?"

"You mean Auntie doesn't have her best friend anymore right next door?" Imani says in a near-whisper.

"No, baby. Auntie doesn't have Miss Ida anymore."

Mommy gets out of the car but she doesn't go around to the trunk to get the suitcases. She just stands at the foot of the three small steps leading to Auntie's walkway, staring at the dark house. Finally she says, "Come on."

They huddle together as Mommy rings the bell, listening for the approach of footsteps. "Did you hear the bell?" Mommy whispers.

"I don't think so, Mommy," Imani says.

"I did," Blair says just to be contrary.

Mommy rings it again and they all bend their heads closer to the door, listening.

Mommy gives it one of those bill-collector knocks. Nothing.

"I don't understand . . ." Mommy almost sounds like a little girl. "Let's look in the side window. Auntie never draws the curtains there."

They creep along the yard. Then Mommy, taking care not to step in Auntie's flower bed, stands on tiptoe to look in Auntie's dining-room window.

"Light's on," she says.

"Do you see Auntie?" Imani asks. "Is she asleep?"

"No. There's no one in there. Maybe we should go around back. Maybe she's in the kitchen with the water running or the radio on and she can't hear us."

They head for the backyard.

"I hope we don't give Auntie a heart attack—creeping around here like this," Mommy says.

Auntie is sitting on her glider, head back, eyes closed. Before anyone can wonder if she's still with the living, she opens her eyes and gives a little start.

"Oh my," she says, putting her hand flat against her

throat. "You all are here already? Oh, I must have fallen asleep." She starts to get up.

"Auntie, what are you doing, sitting out here in the dark?" Mommy asks.

Auntie smooths down the skirt of her housecoat. She has on her old blue terry house shoes. Now Auntie looks up at the sky.

"I was just out here looking up at that big ol' straw-berry moon. Thinkin' about that time I told you about it. You remember, Junie?"

Auntie is the only one who still calls Mommy Junie. She's June to everyone else. She's been June since college.

"I remember. But what are you doing back here?" Imani's mother looks at the front-porch glider that is now on the back porch.

"Can't sit on the front porch no more. Had to have my glider moved back here. Nobody can hang out in front of their house these days after dark. Too much of that gang activity."

Imani senses her mother's grim thoughts as they follow Auntie into the kitchen.

"Auntie, you should move from this place. They have a nice retirement home off Crenshaw, behind the mall."

"Oh, no. I'd never leave this street. This is my home. We all got enough changes to put up with. Why would I want to bring one on my own self? Besides, how could I just move away? I still have friends on this street. What

would Mr. Bell do if I wasn't here to help him sort through his bills or remind him about his blood pressure medicine?"

Mommy sighs and Imani knows she is sighing for patience. Auntie pulls out a chair for Mommy at the table and they all sit down while she goes to the cabinet for plates.

As she sets the plates and forks down on the table, she says, "Did your mama tell you the story about how the Indians saw time? About the strawberry moon? Why I told her about it?" Auntie is changing the subject.

"She told me," says Imani.

Blair lays his head on his folded arms. In a muffled voice he says, "Imani said I was born during the month of the worm moon!"

Auntie looks over at him and her eyes get big. "That's right. You were born in March."

He nods sleepily.

Auntie laughs. "Well, that's the month of the sugar moon, too. So you can claim either one of those you want. It's up to you."

"I was born during the month of the sugar moon." Blair raises his head to make the announcement.

"Yes." She bends down to give him a hug. "You're as sweet as sugar." Auntie sits and begins to cut the cake. Mommy passes out the napkins. "The last time your mommy and I sat on that porch looking up at the

strawberry moon, she was just getting ready to go with her mother. And she didn't want to go."

Imani whips around to look at her mother. This is the first she's heard that Mommy hadn't wanted to go with her own mother. All those stories were about her longing for her mother.

"They weren't going far," Auntie says. "Just out to Compton. They were building new houses out there then and with your daddy's GI Bill . . . Your mama and her brother, Junior, and her mother and father were going to get one of those nice new homes. But suddenly, Junie just didn't want to go.

"For days I'd catch her watching her mother. When her mother was painting her nails or showing Junie a new blouse she'd bought for a job interview, I could tell your mama was watching her mother—for a sign."

"What kind of sign?" Imani asks. She looks at her mother closely.

"That she was going to up and leave her."

As if she is talking about someone else, someone not sitting there at the table with them, Auntie says, "One day Junie just took off. Did your mommy ever tell you all that story?"

"No," Imani says, turning to fully face her mother. Mommy looks as if she is remembering it only just then.

"You didn't tell them about that, Junie—the time you ran away?"

"No, I didn't tell them that one, Auntie," Imani's mother says, and though she seems saddened in a long-ago way, she doesn't make any noises of resistance. She just sits back, ready to listen to that story along with Imani and Blair. This gives Auntie the go-ahead.

Auntie starts right in. "We didn't even know Junie was gone. For a long time. Most of that morning, I think. It was a Saturday. Until her mother called her in for a chore. Her daddy had gone out to buy a new color television and her mother was packing up their things. She wanted Junie to vacuum the room that had been hers all year. I think that's what it was." Auntie stops a moment to ponder this.

"I thought you were outside someplace lying on the grass, staring up at the clouds like you always were doin' when you wanted to think. But you weren't out back. Then I called over to Miss Ida's to see if you were there pestering her. But no, you weren't there neither."

Imani's mouth has dropped open with interest. Blair's as well. Mommy just stares down at her hands, a little smile on her face.

"My goodness. By that time your mother was getting a little nervous. We both walked over to . . ." Auntie turns to Mommy. "What was that little girl's name? That little friend of yours?"

"Renee," Mommy says.

"Oh, right. We walked over to her house. Didn't know

her phone number. But you weren't there neither. We even went next door to that other little girl's house." Auntie squints trying to remember. "You know, that little hateful child."

"Rhonda," Mommy says.

"Oh, that was a hateful child. Your mama tell you all the hateful stuff she used to do?"

Imani grins with guilty pleasure. "She told us."

"Course your mama wasn't at Rhonda's." Auntie stops. Her eyes widen. "Wait a minute! You know what I heard just the other day? I was down at the farmer's market— you know they have that in the parking lot back behind the old Hub's furniture store—and I ran into my friend Rae Gardner. Seems her grandson is in that Rhonda girl's first-grade class. Seems she's been teaching first grade for years. I told my friend Rae, 'Honey, I don't know how she is now, but that was one mean little girl your grandbaby has for a teacher.' And you know what my friend Rae said? 'Oh, Mrs. Johnson's nice as pie.' You just don't know how things are gonna turn out, do you?"

"Auntie, I just can't picture Rhonda turning out to be a nice person," Mommy says.

"So what happened, Auntie—to Mommy?" Imani asks a little impatiently.

"Oh yes," Auntie said. "Well, by then we were getting pretty worried. Your mama's daddy came home and he wasn't worried at first—nor your great-uncle Melvin nei-

ther, God rest his soul—but as it grew later and the sun started going down, he finally got worried enough to call the police. Your mama's daddy, that is."

"Your mama was the sweetest thing." Auntie seems to be getting off track again. "You know what she told me when we found her?"

"Found her where, Auntie? Where had she gone?" Now it's as if Mommy isn't even sitting there.

"I'm getting to that." Auntie takes a deep breath. "Your mama had walked all the way down to Santa Barbara— it's Martin Luther King Boulevard now—and Western to that police station that's still there, don't you know. Well, she didn't go to the police station exactly, she went to the laundry-mat across the street from it. So by the time her daddy called the police and described what she was wearing, one of the officers who'd been to the Winchell's next door—"

"Winchell's?" Imani asks.

"Doughnuts. Anyway, your mama, who was always the scaredest little thing, hadn't thought her bright idea through. Where was she going to go? What was she going to eat? And she was too afraid of being kidnapped to go very far. So she thought she'd just live in the laundry-mat across from the police station."

"I didn't think anything of the sort," Mommy says.

"Well, what were you thinking?"

"I honestly don't remember. It was a stupid thing to do.

*I don't even know why I did it. I just remember being
afraid. Of the unknown and things I couldn't control."*

*"When her daddy called and described to the police
the clothes your mama was last seen wearing . . . Oh boy,
did her mother ever burst into tears when she heard your
mama's daddy describing the pedal pushers and sandals
and sleeveless pullover."*

Mommy looks surprised at that.

*"The policeman said he'd spotted a little girl sitting
there in the laundry-mat, seemingly all alone—just sitting there with a little brown stuffed dog that looked like
most of the stuffing was out. Then we knew it was you,
Junie. And we said, 'Could you just bring her over to the
police station and we'll come and get her. Her daddy will
be right down.'*

*"He brought you back"—Auntie is talking directly to
Mommy now—"and you looked so embarrassed. After
your daddy brought you home, your mother was so mad
she could spit, so she said, 'Dot—you deal with her.'*

*"Junie told me—and it was the sweetest thing: 'I don't
want to leave you, Auntie. Because I know I can count
on you. I'm not sure anymore what my mother will do. I
try to be sure. But I'm not. I thought if I ran away, she'd
be so mad, she'd let me stay with you.' "*

*"I said that?" Mommy frowns as if she doesn't remem-
ber.*

"You sure did. What did I tell you, Junie?"

"I don't remember."

"Ain't none of us perfect. Only God's perfect."

"I remember that," Mommy says slowly.

"Everybody lets somebody down at one time or another. But your family, Junie, was your mother and your father and your hardheaded brother." Auntie sits back. "I think I reached you."

"You always reached me, Auntie."

"We went out to look up at the moon that night. It was a full strawberry moon. Like tonight. God's beautiful creation. You began to calm down. We could sit out front during that time. On summer nights Browning Avenue would be full of kids running up and down and people on their porches shouting across to each other or down to each other . . ." Auntie has switched subjects. They are all silent, imagining or remembering that other time.

Imani can't finish her cake. She pushes the plate little by little away from her. Blair's eyes are closed. He's fallen asleep. Imani reaches into her pocket, secretly, and feels the folded piece of paper she's had there the whole trip. Daddy's new phone number—copied from the phone bill Imani found in Mommy's desk drawer. All day and part of the night Imani has been smug in the knowledge it was there—in her pocket. And she's known that as soon as she could, maybe after everyone had gone to sleep, she was going to sneak into the kitchen and figure out how to work Auntie's telephone with the rotary dial. It should be easy enough. She was going to call her daddy and tell him to come get her as soon as he could. She'd understand if it was going to take a few days.

She was going to tell him she wanted to be with him, at least for the summer. But now she knows she won't. Maybe in a couple of weeks, but not now. Mommy's going to need her, for a little while.

"It's not like that nowadays," Auntie was saying. "The day you moved, Junie—don't you remember how you were going down the walkway and you didn't even look back? I was kind of hurt, but I knew that's how you had to do it. I knew I was going to see you often, because it wasn't like you were moving across the country. But I saw those little shoulders of yours kind of hunched and defeated and determined and courageous all at the same time, like you were going off to war, and I said a special prayer that night for you and I knew you were going to be okay."

Imani watches as Mommy reaches across the table to get Imani's plate. She can't let Auntie's Sock-It-to-Me cake go to waste.